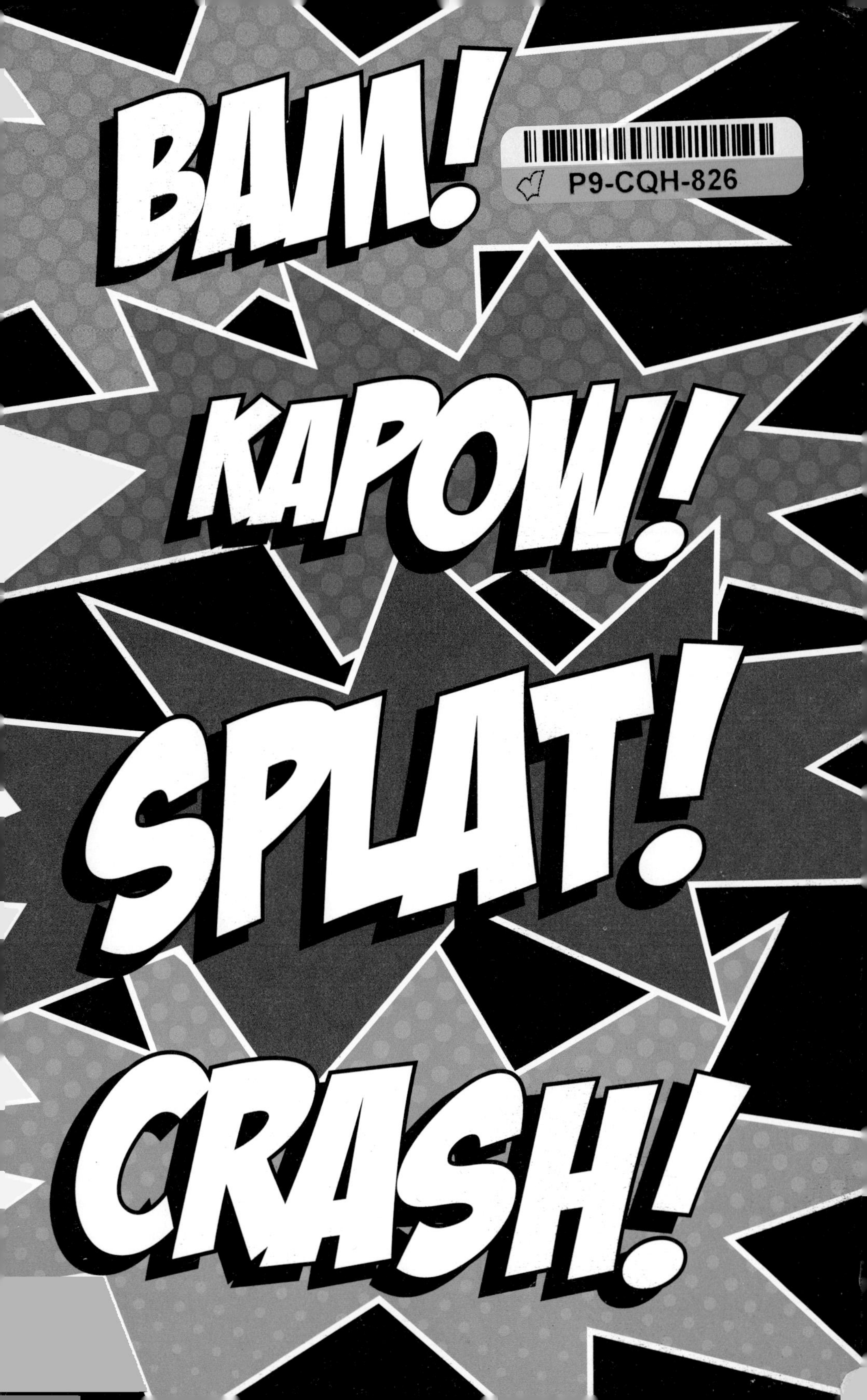
BAM!
KAPOW!
SPLAT!
CRASH!

LEGO

DC UNIVERSE™
SUPER HEROES

HANDBOOK

SCHOLASTIC INC.

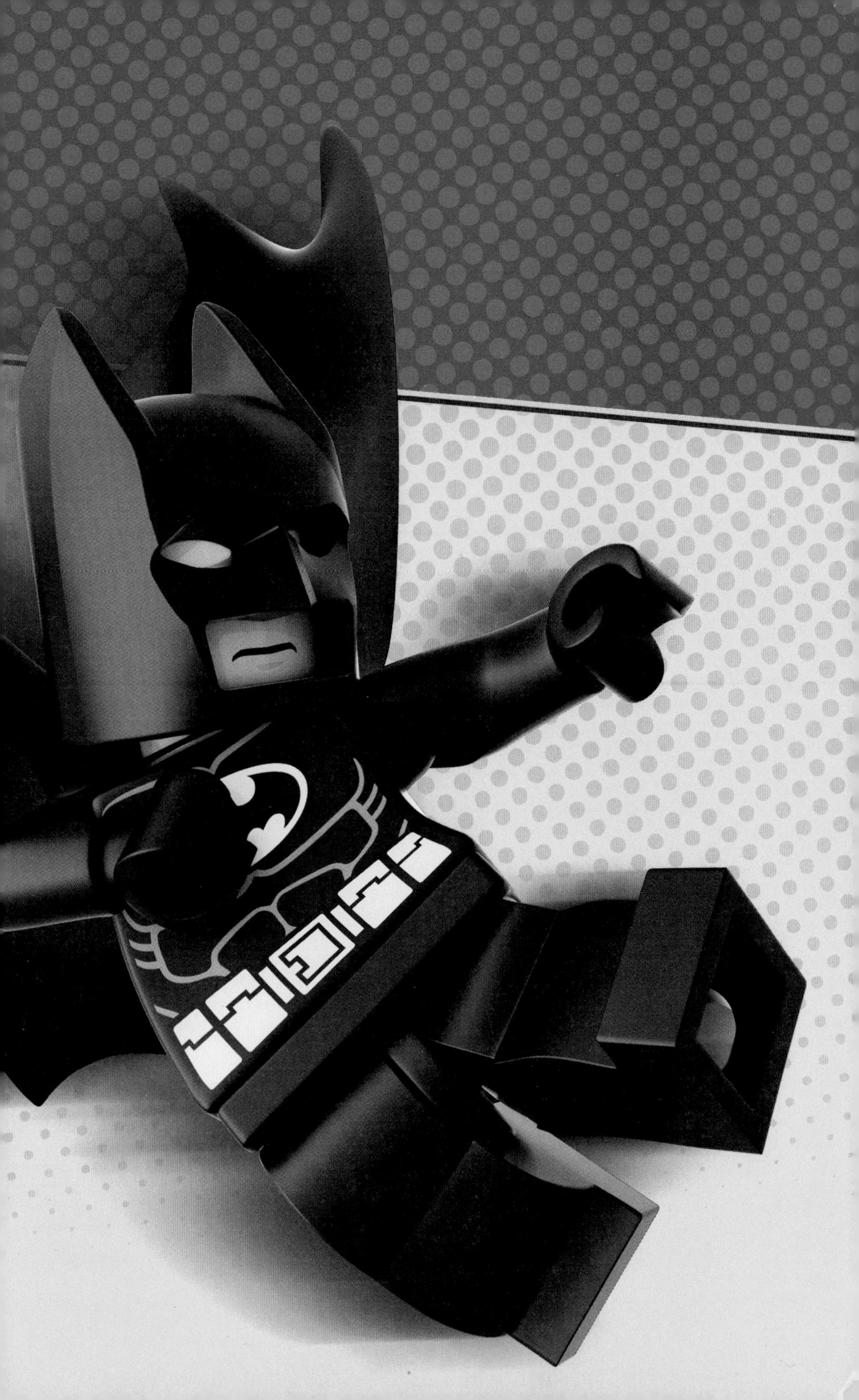

ISBN 978-0-545-55225-7

12 11 10 9 8 7 6 5 4 3 2 1   13 14 15 16 17 18/0
Printed in the U.S.A.   40
First printing, June 2013

TABLE OF CONTENTS

INTRODUCTION

The DC Universe features some of the most famous and incredible super heroes and super-villains ever created. Now these amazing fighters for justice and their archenemies have become LEGO® Minifigures. In this book, we'll take a look at the heroes and villains, as well as their unique histories, vehicles, weapons, and locations. You may even discover some secrets about the characters themselves!

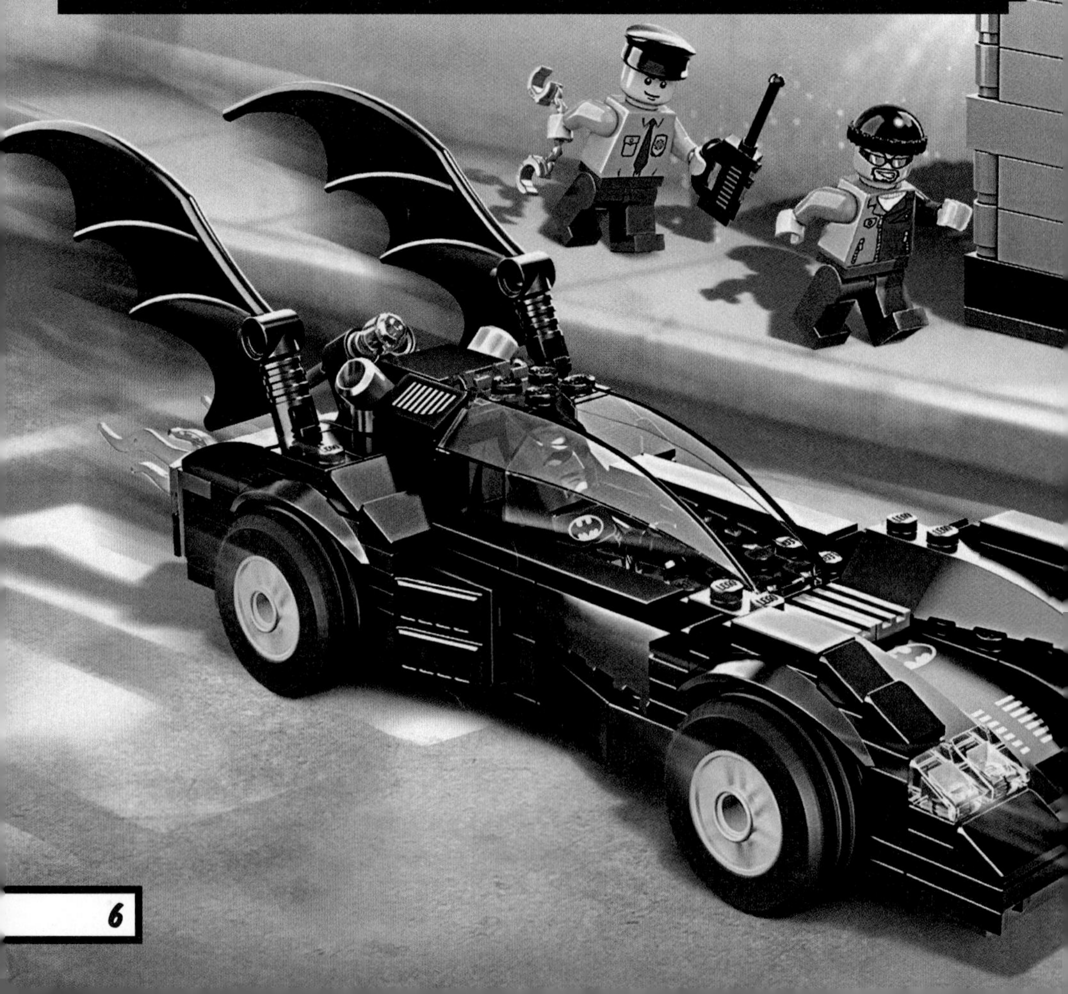

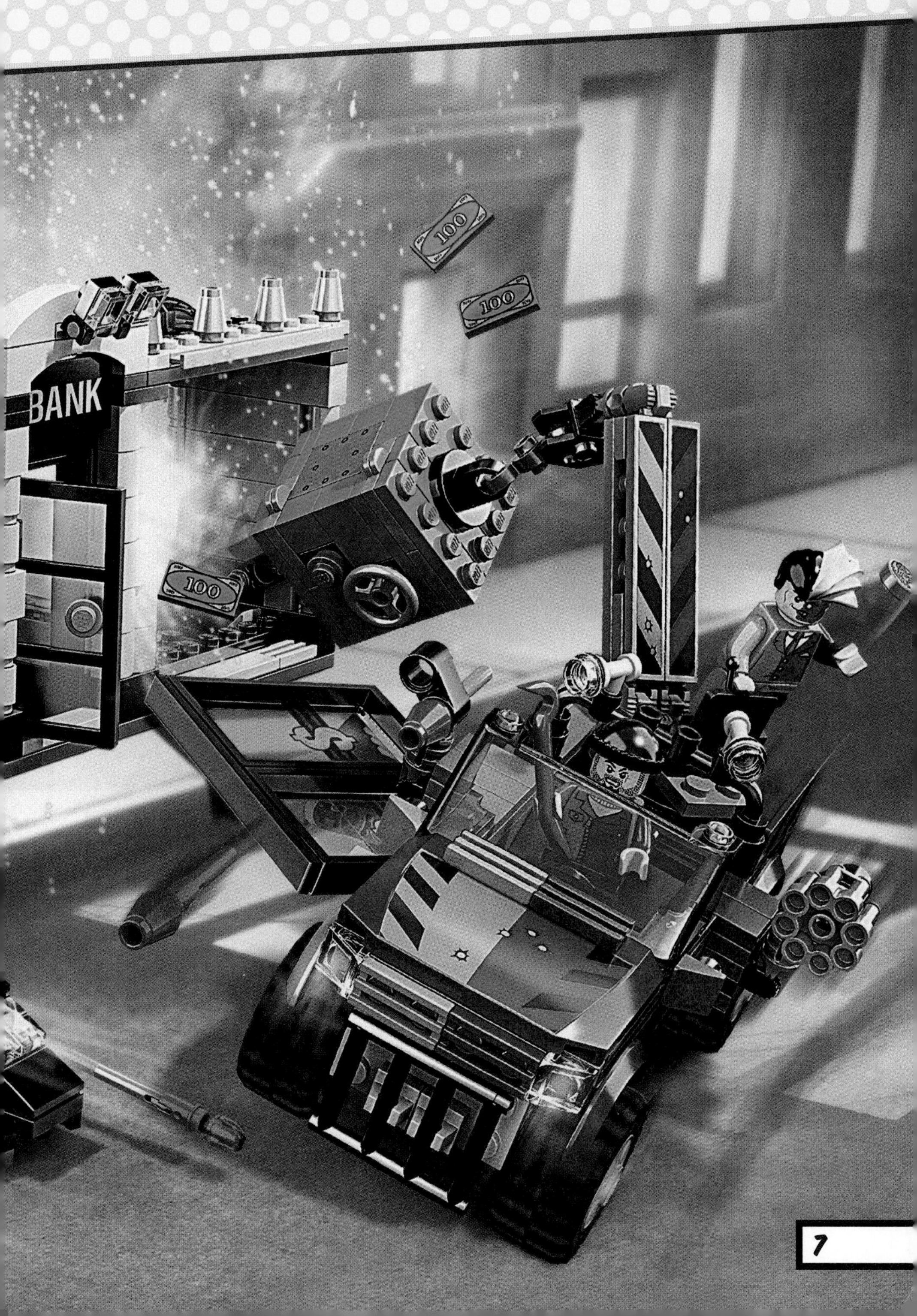
BANK
100
100
100

CHAPTER 1
SUPER

HEROES!

IT DOESN'T MATTER IF THEY ARE AN ALIEN, AN AMAZON PRINCESS, THE KING OF THE SEVEN SEAS, OR THE WORLD'S GREATEST DETECTIVE, THE WORLD RELIES ON THEM TO KEEP IT SAFE. NO MATTER WHAT THE DANGER, THEY ARE THERE, FIGHTING THE WORLD'S DEADLIEST VILLAINS. ALONE OR TOGETHER, THEY ARE THE MOST POWERFUL FORCES FOR GOOD THAT EARTH HAS EVER SEEN.

SUPERMAN

Superman is the most powerful super hero in the universe. He is a champion of truth and justice, and uses his mighty powers only in the cause of good. He makes his home in the city of **Metropolis**, but fights menaces anywhere in the world and even in outer space.

Born on the planet **Krypton**, the baby who would grow up to be Superman was sent to Earth in a rocket by his parents just before his homeworld exploded. Arriving on Earth, he was found and adopted by a kindly couple, the **Kents**. They named him **Clark Kent** and taught him to use his powers for the cause of justice.

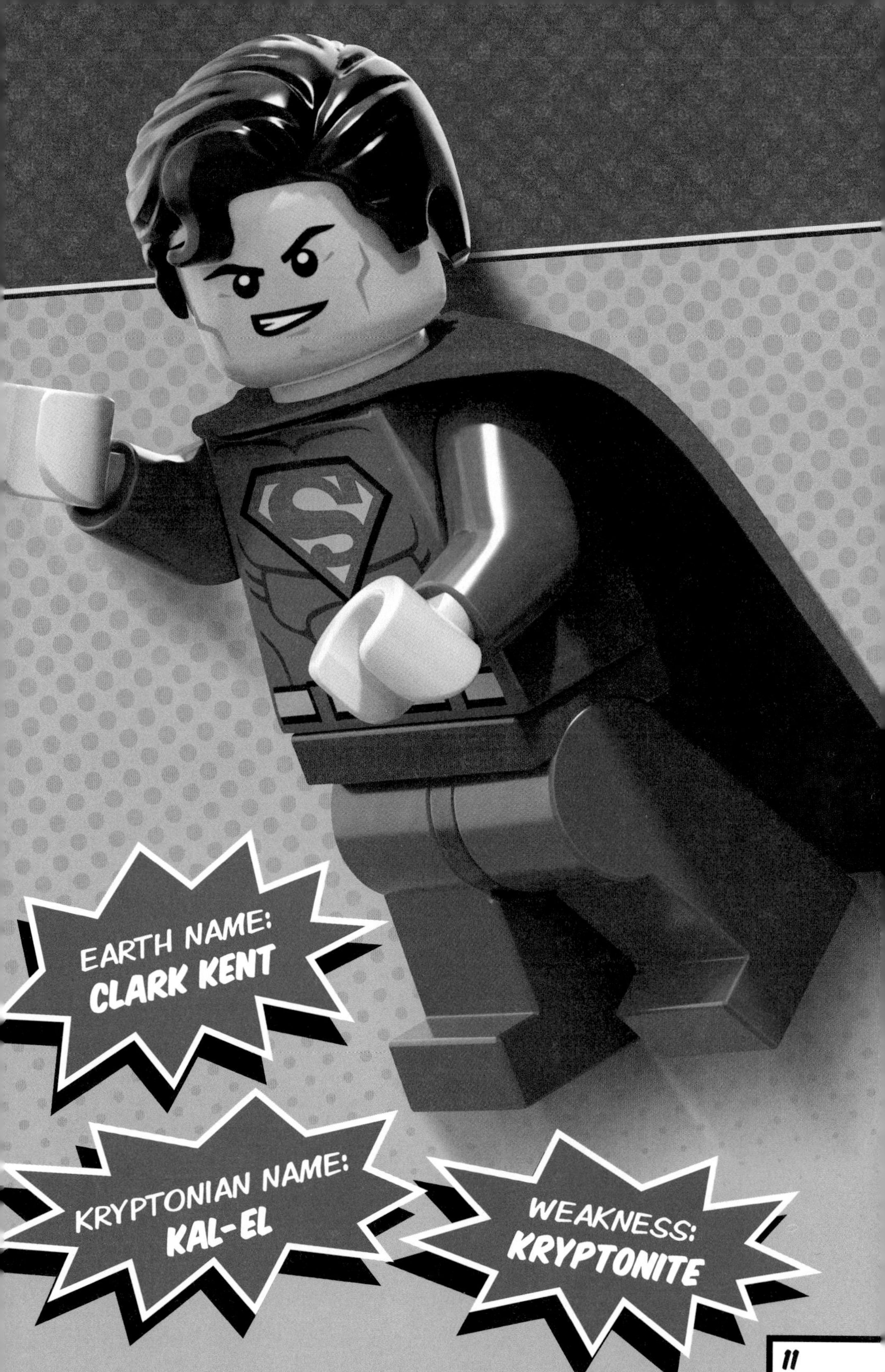
EARTH NAME:
CLARK KENT
KRYPTONIAN NAME:
KAL-EL
WEAKNESS:
KRYPTONITE

SUPERMAN

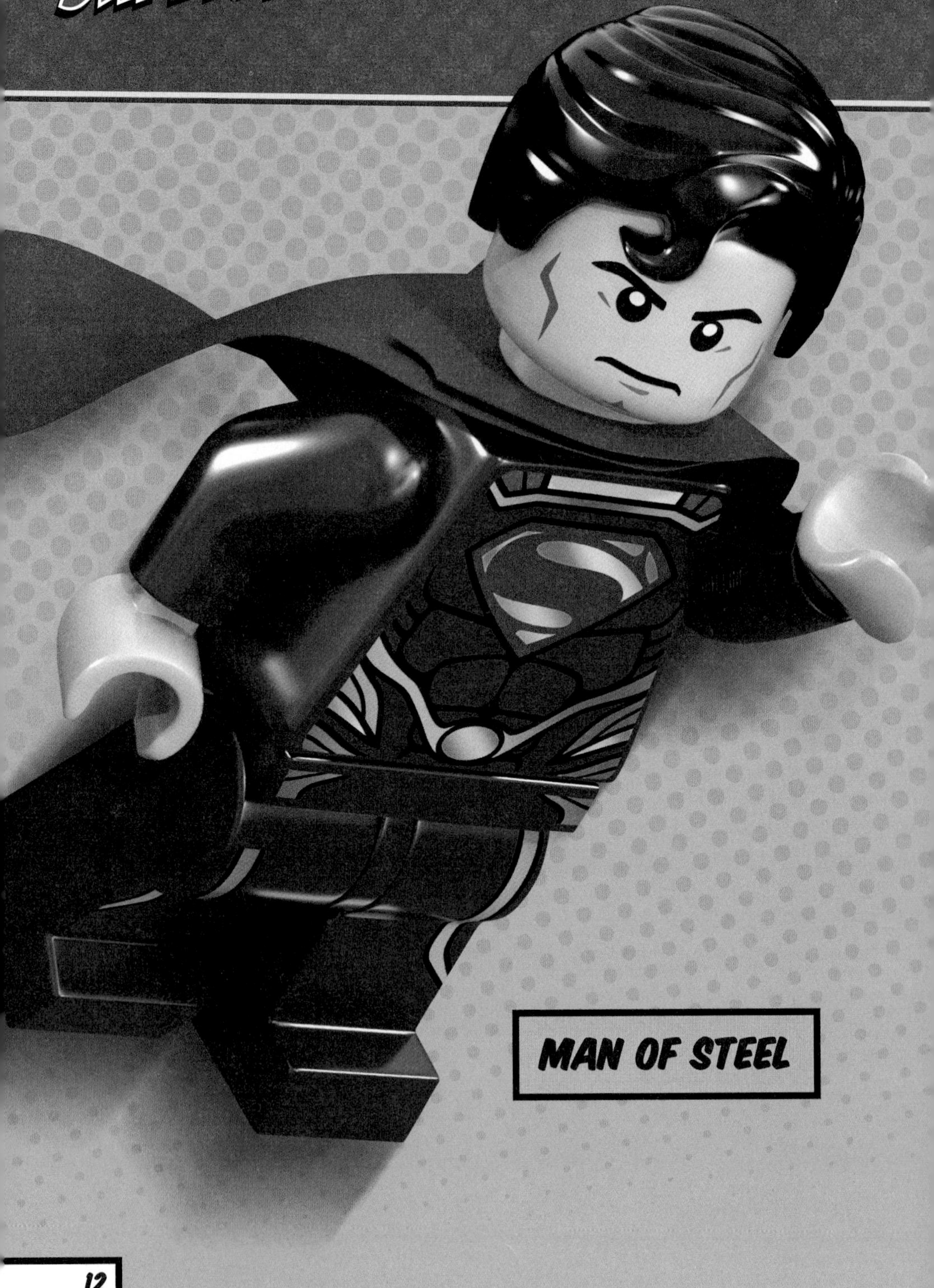

MAN OF STEEL

Superman has many powers. He gets much of his strength from the rays of Earth's yellow sun, and loses his powers under a red sun.

When Krypton exploded, the fragments of the planet became a radioactive element called **Kryptonite**. The radiation from Kryptonite can cause great harm to Superman. Villains (like **Lex Luthor**) have often used Kryptonite against the Man of Steel. Superman is also vulnerable to magic.

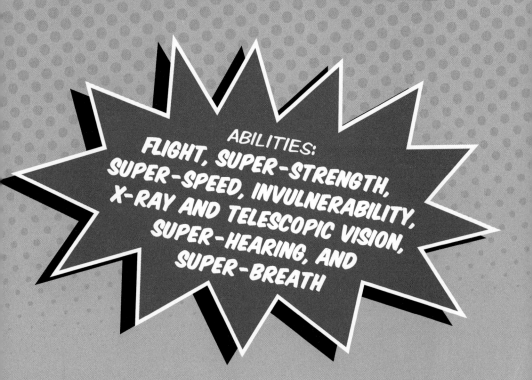

ABILITIES:
FLIGHT, SUPER-STRENGTH, SUPER-SPEED, INVULNERABILITY, X-RAY AND TELESCOPIC VISION, SUPER-HEARING, AND SUPER-BREATH

BATMAN

Batman made a life-long vow to fight for law and order, and to stop all criminals. Although he has no special powers like Superman or the Flash, he uses his fighting skills and his brain to defeat some of the worst villains in the DC Universe.

His secret identity is **Bruce Wayne**, the richest man in Gotham City. Only a few people know that beneath Wayne Manor is the amazing **Batcave**, Batman's headquarters. When danger threatens, Bruce Wayne puts on the cape and cowl of the Dark Knight and rushes to the rescue.

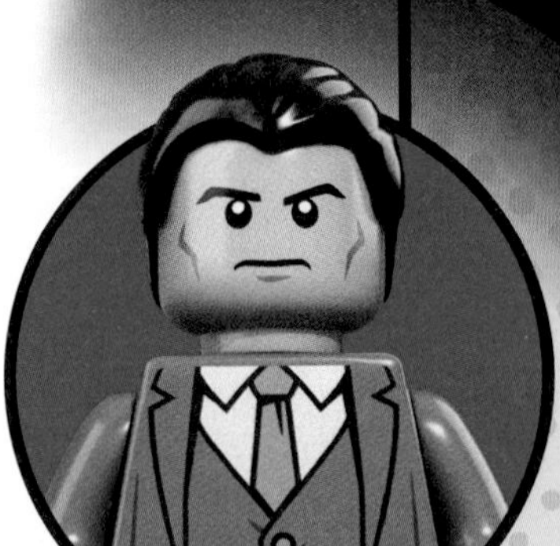

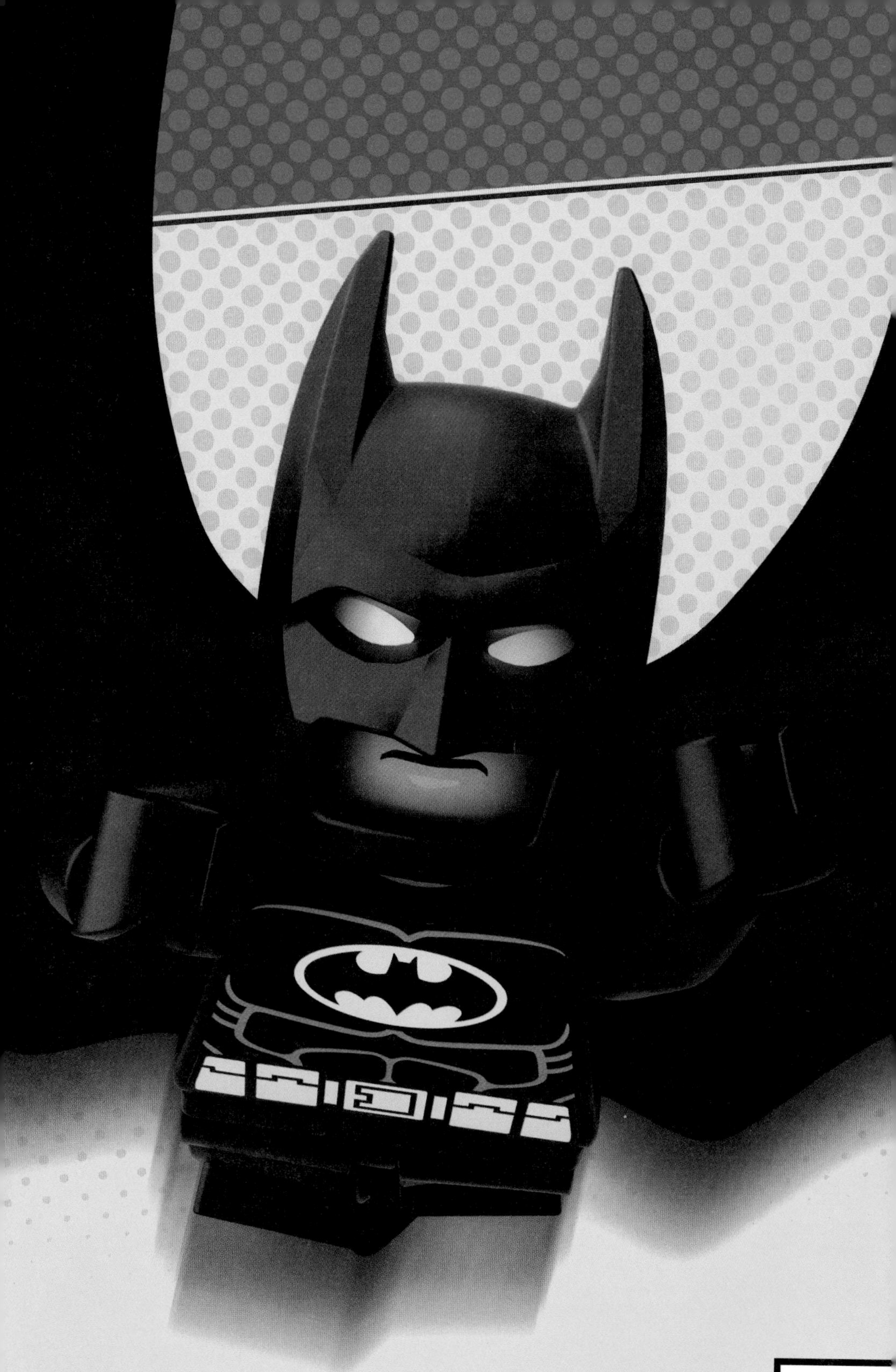

BATMAN

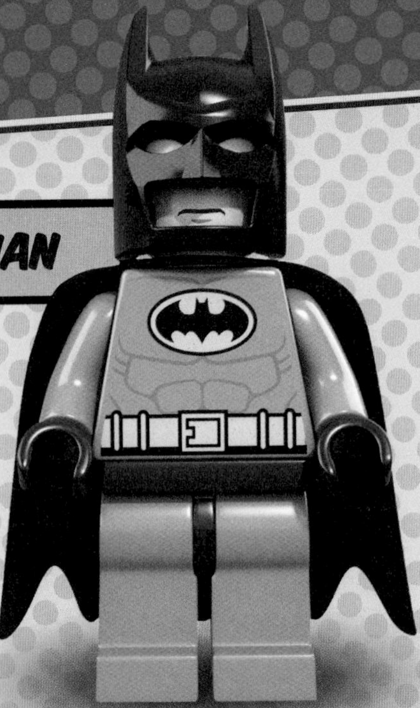

CLASSIC BATMAN

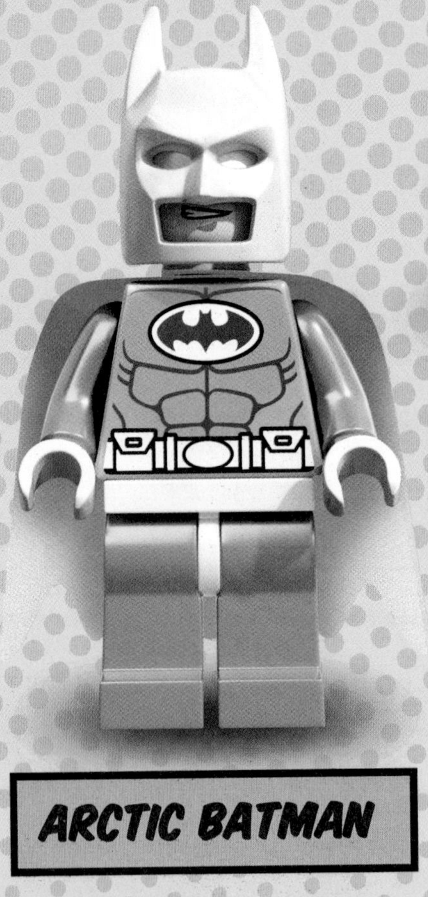

ARCTIC BATMAN

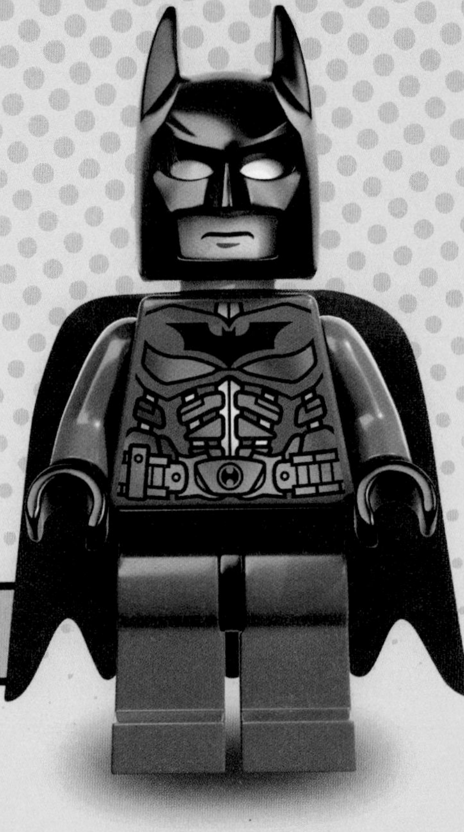

DARK KNIGHT

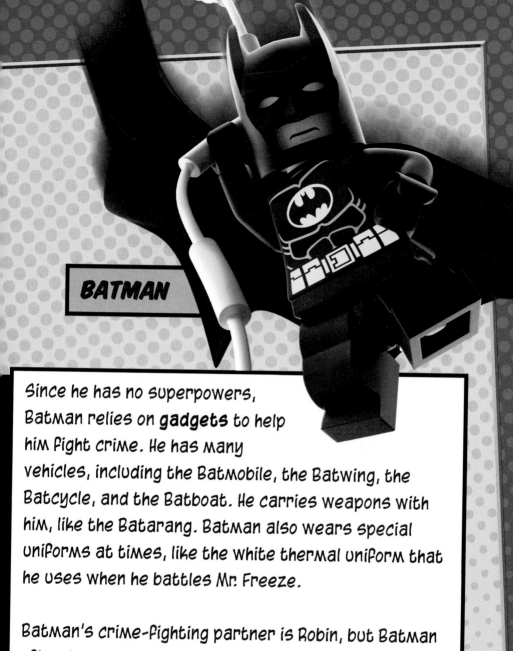

BATMAN

Since he has no superpowers, Batman relies on **gadgets** to help him fight crime. He has many vehicles, including the Batmobile, the Batwing, the Batcycle, and the Batboat. He carries weapons with him, like the Batarang. Batman also wears special uniforms at times, like the white thermal uniform that he uses when he battles Mr. Freeze.

Batman's crime-fighting partner is Robin, but Batman often teams up with Superman, Wonder Woman, the Flash, and other heroes. They are always amazed by all he is able to accomplish **without superpowers**. No matter the challenge, Batman will find a way to keep **Gotham City** safe.

ROBIN

Batman's partner, Robin, is a young crime fighter who also solves cases on his own. He combines **computer genius** with **martial arts** training he received from Batman, resulting in a double threat to the criminals of Gotham City. Robin is a master of many weapons.

REAL NAME:
TIM DRAKE

EQUIPMENT:
KENDO STICK; GRAPNEL GUN

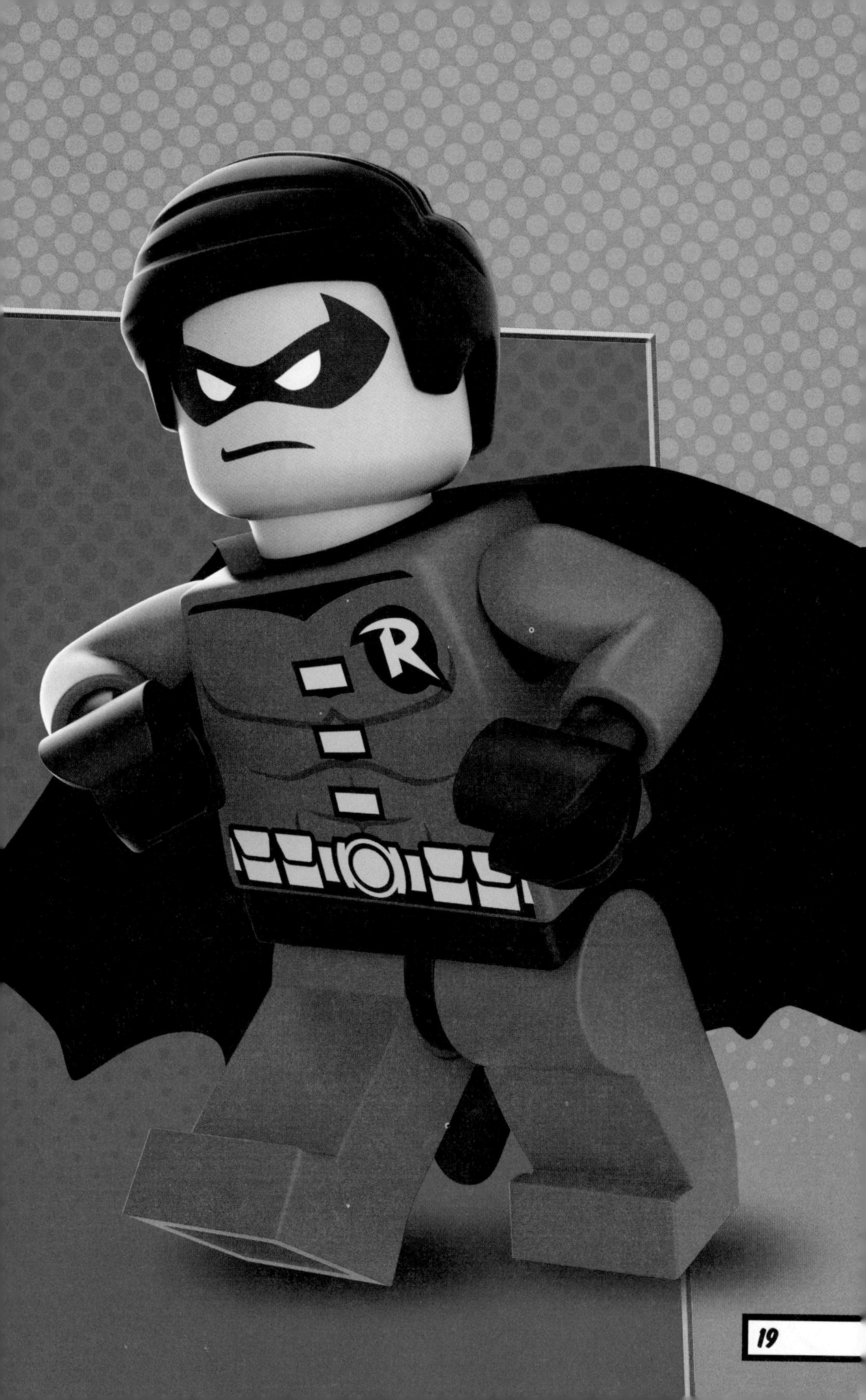

WONDER WOMAN

Princess Diana of the **Amazons** is on a mission to promote peace and understanding between all peoples. Unfortunately, the world is full of villains and Diana, as Wonder Woman, has to fight to protect the innocent. With **super-strength** and **super-speed**, she is only surpassed by Superman for sheer power. She also carries a **Golden Lasso of Truth**, which makes anyone caught in it answer any question truthfully.

REAL NAME:
PRINCESS DIANA OF THEMYSCIRA (ALSO GOES BY DIANA PRINCE)

EQUIPMENT:
BULLETPROOF BRACELETS; GOLDEN LASSO OF TRUTH

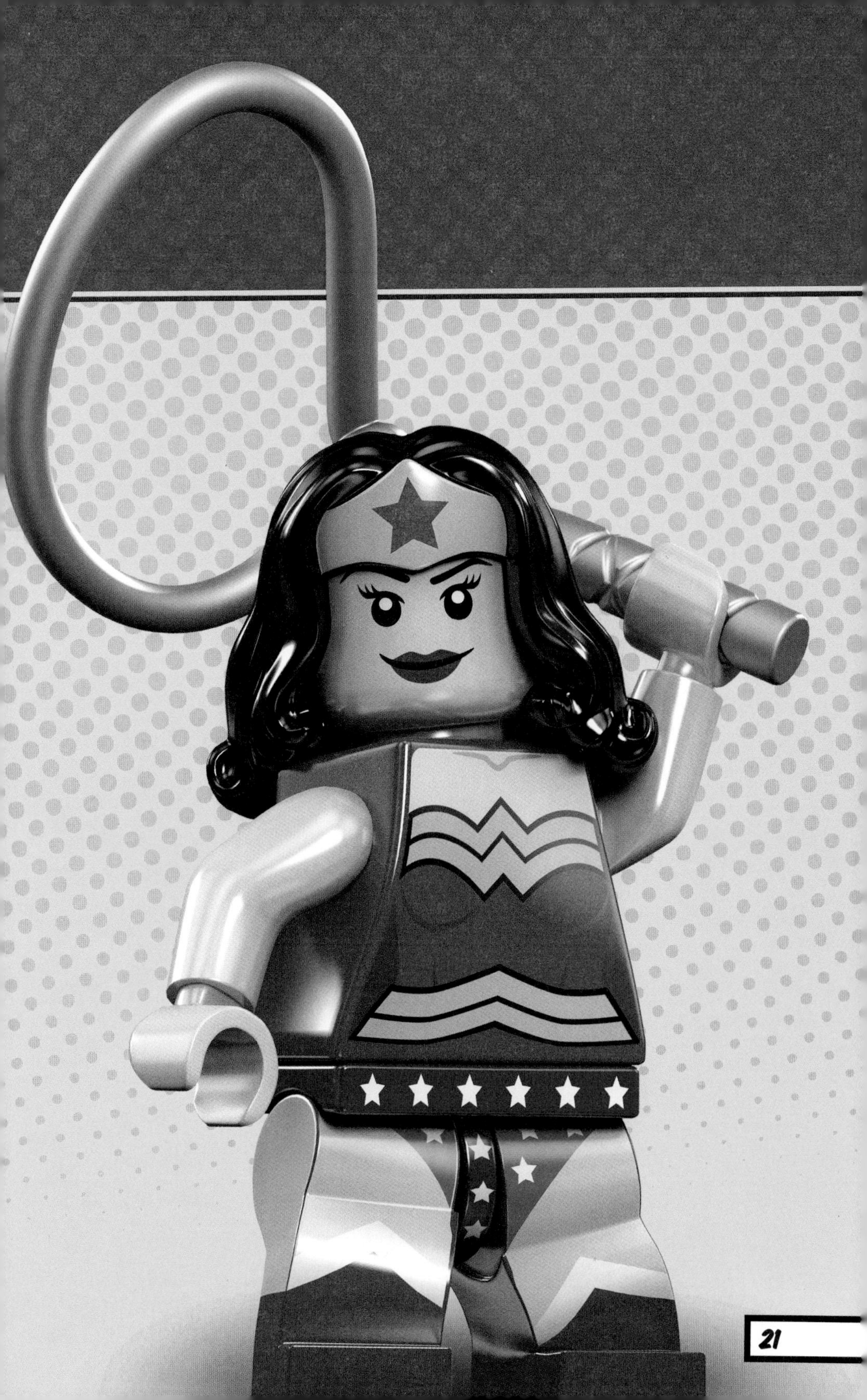

AQUAMAN

King of **Atlantis** and master of the Seven Seas, Aquaman is able to **breathe underwater** and **command sea life** by transmitting his thoughts to them. He can swim as fast as 100 miles per hour. He has **super-strength** and great endurance, along with enormous knowledge about the ocean and everything that lives in it.

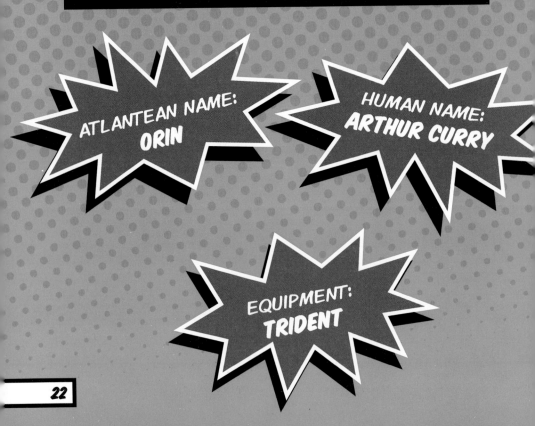

ATLANTEAN NAME: **ORIN**

HUMAN NAME: **ARTHUR CURRY**

EQUIPMENT: **TRIDENT**

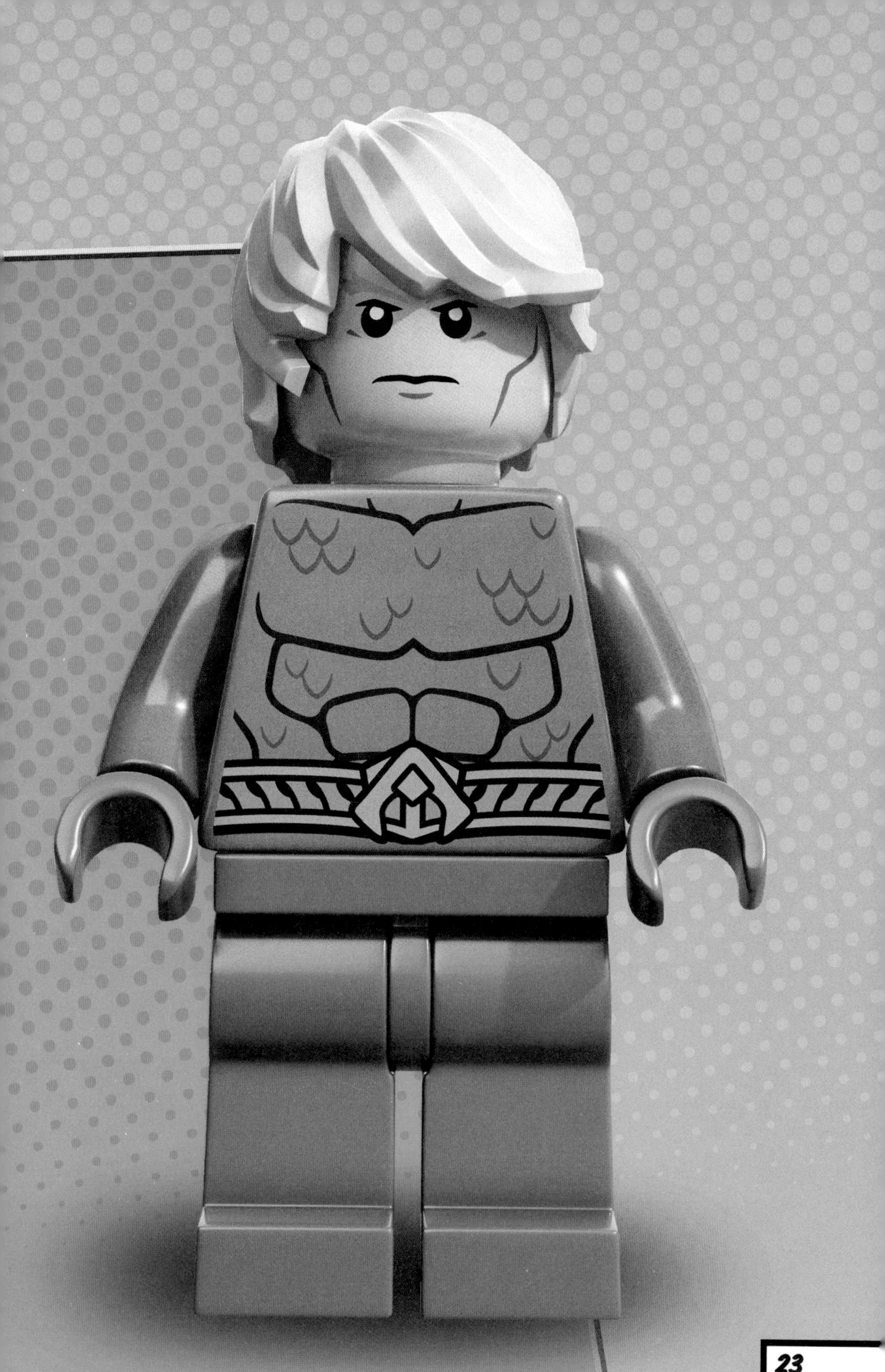

THE FLASH

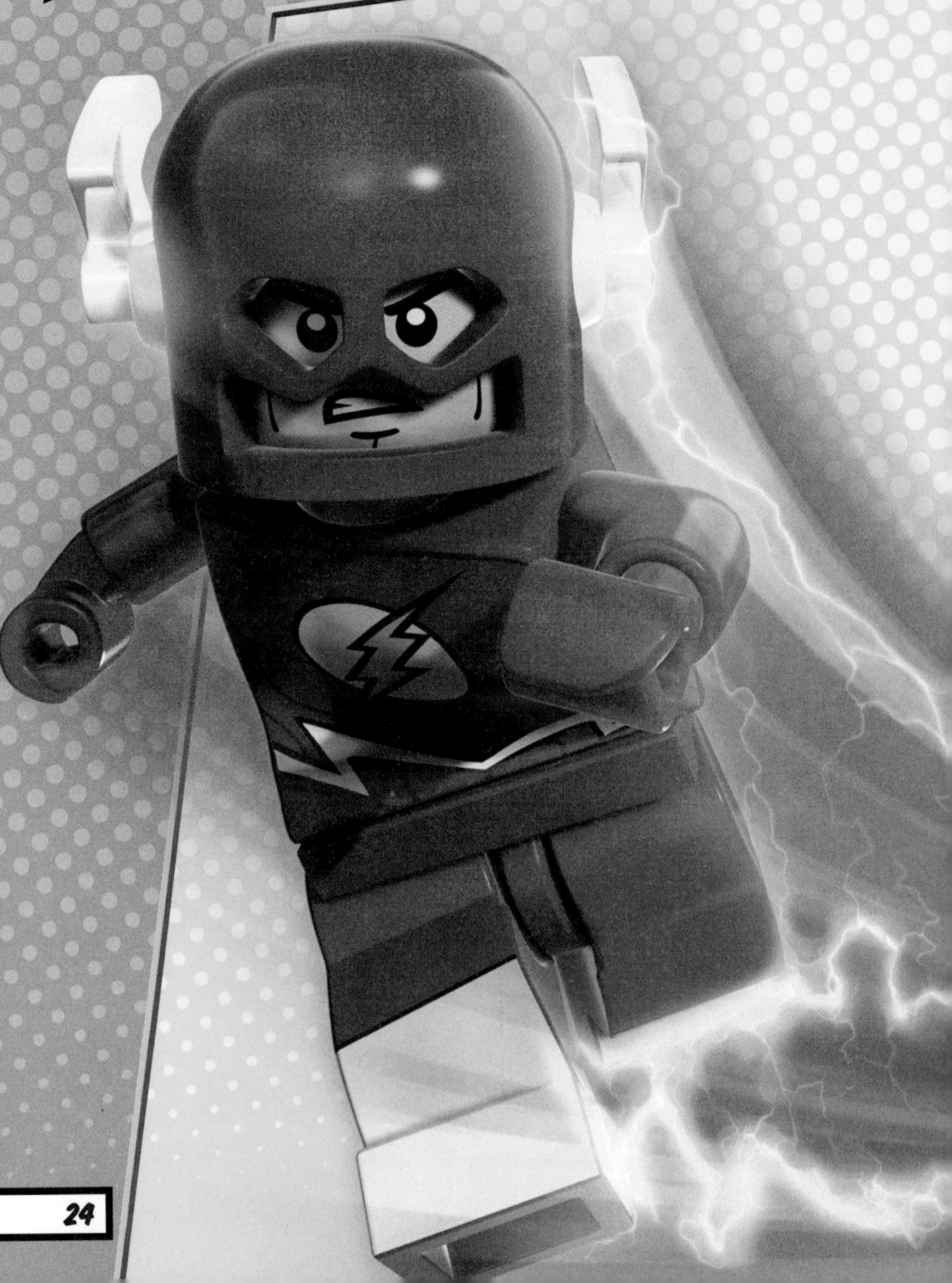

The Flash can run at close to the **speed of light**, pass through solid objects, race up the sides of buildings, and even **phase into other dimensions**. He can subdue villains in hundreds of different ways, from running around them so fast that he creates a vacuum to sending them hurtling up to the sky with a mini-tornado.

REAL NAME:
BARRY ALLEN

EQUIPMENT:
THE FLASH DOESN'T NEED ANY SPECIAL TOOLS, BUT WHEN HE IS BARRY ALLEN HE WEARS A RING THAT CONTAINS HIS COSTUME!

GREEN LANTERN

Green Lantern Hal Jordan is a member of a huge organization of heroes from countless worlds throughout the universe. He gains his superpowers from a **green power ring**. Jordan quickly discovered that his ring enabled him to **fly** and to create anything he imagined out of **green energy**, from a shield against bullets to a giant hammer. The ring needs to be recharged every twenty-four hours.

REAL NAME:
HAL JORDAN

ABILITIES:
THOUGH HIS GREEN LANTERN RING GIVES HIM GREAT POWERS, IT ONLY WORKS BECAUSE OF HIS WILLPOWER.

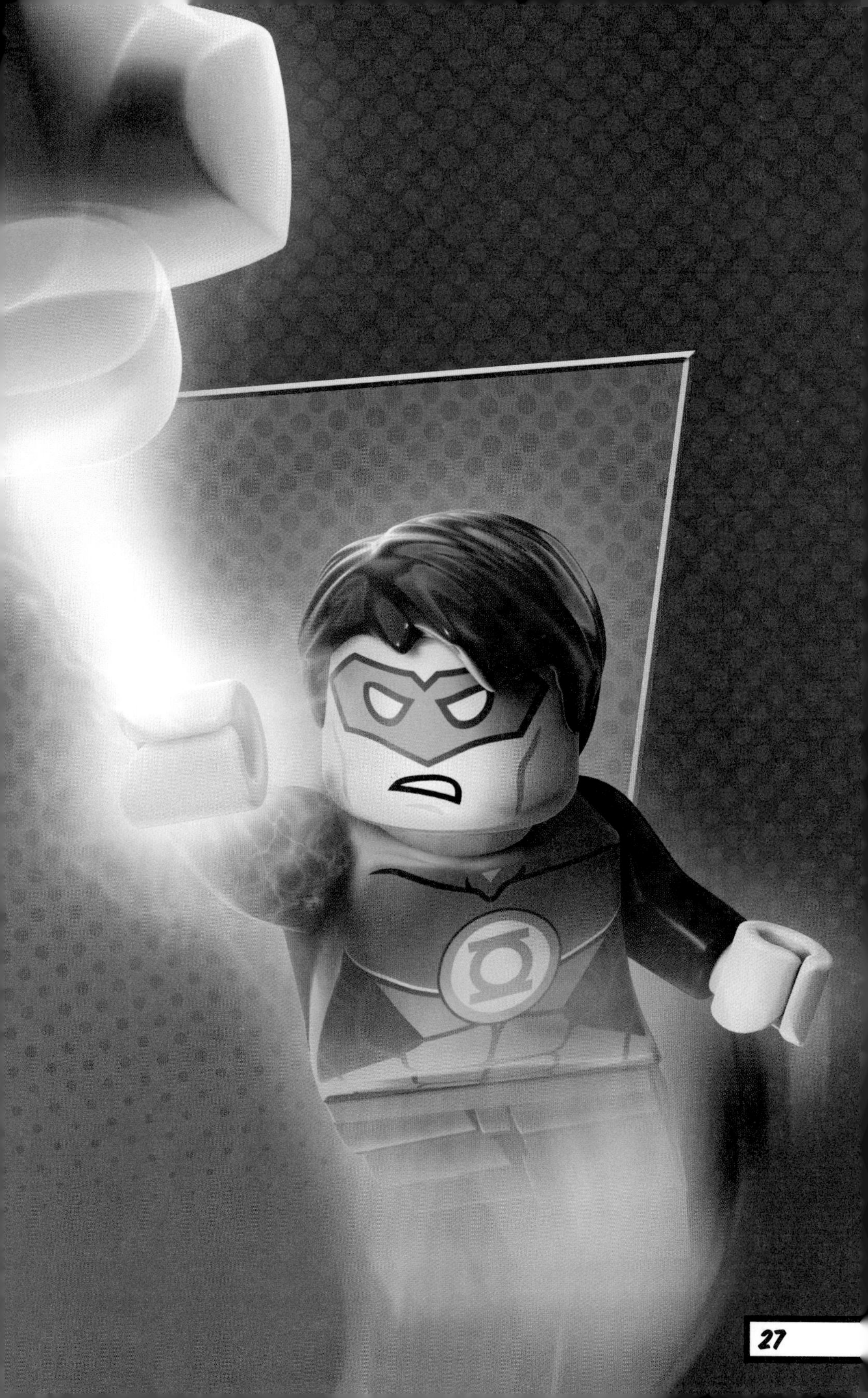

COMMISSIONER GORDON

James Gordon is the commissioner of police in **Gotham City**. He was the first important city official to work with Batman and trust the masked hero. Thanks to Gordon, Batman became a valuable ally of the police. **Honest**, **smart**, and **loyal**, Gordon is Batman's best friend on the police force. Together, they fight to keep the people of Gotham City safe from crime.

EQUIPMENT: GUN; WALKIE-TALKIE; HANDCUFFS

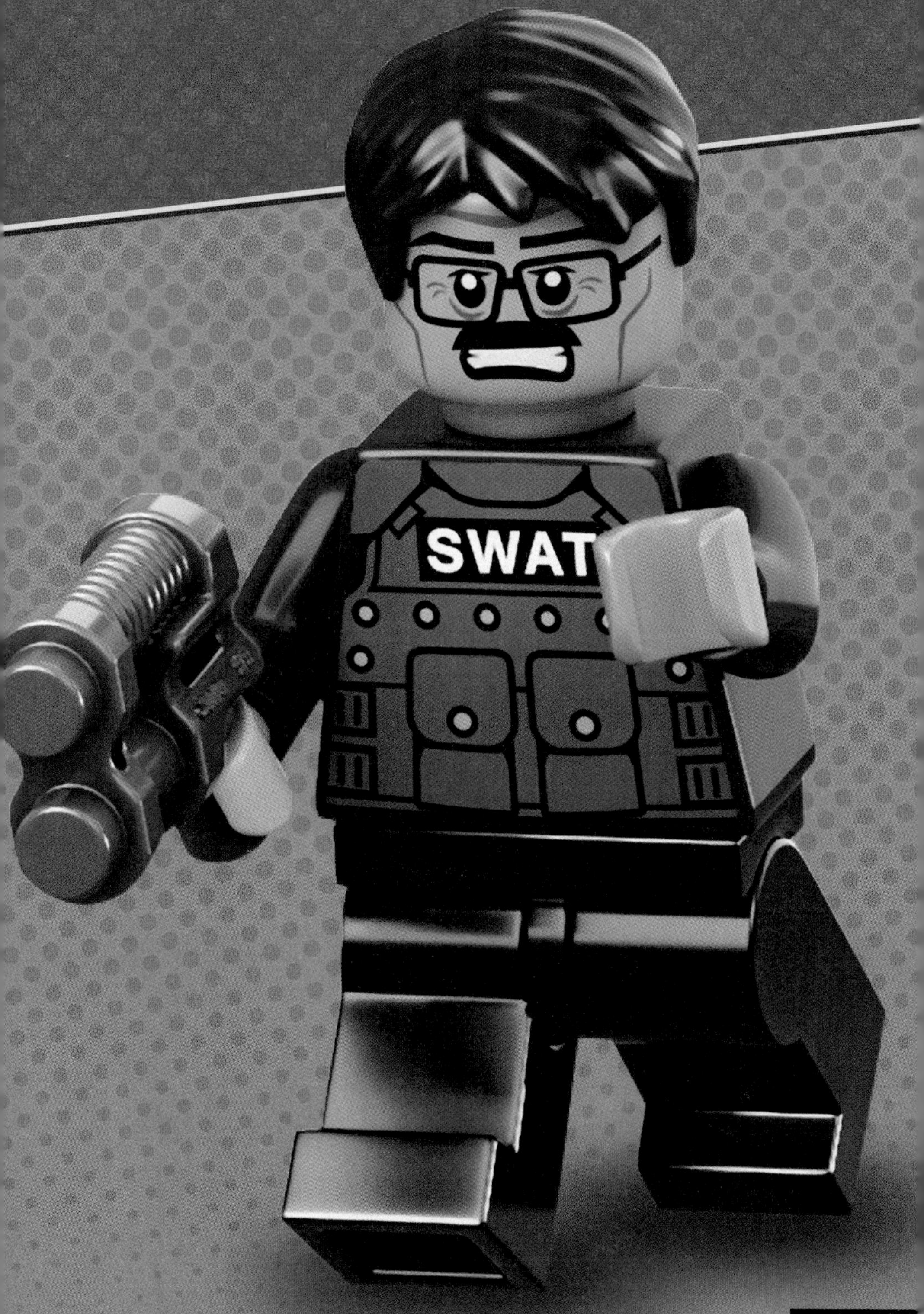
SWAT

LOIS LANE

Lois Lane is a **reporter** for the *Daily Planet*, the largest newspaper in the city of **Metropolis**. Lane is dedicated to her job and incredibly brave, to the point of being reckless at times. More than once, she has found herself in danger while pursuing a story, only to be saved by Superman. At the same time, information she has dug up has often **helped Superman** solve mysteries.

ABILITIES:
COURAGE TO REPORT THE WHOLE STORY—NO MATTER THE DANGER.

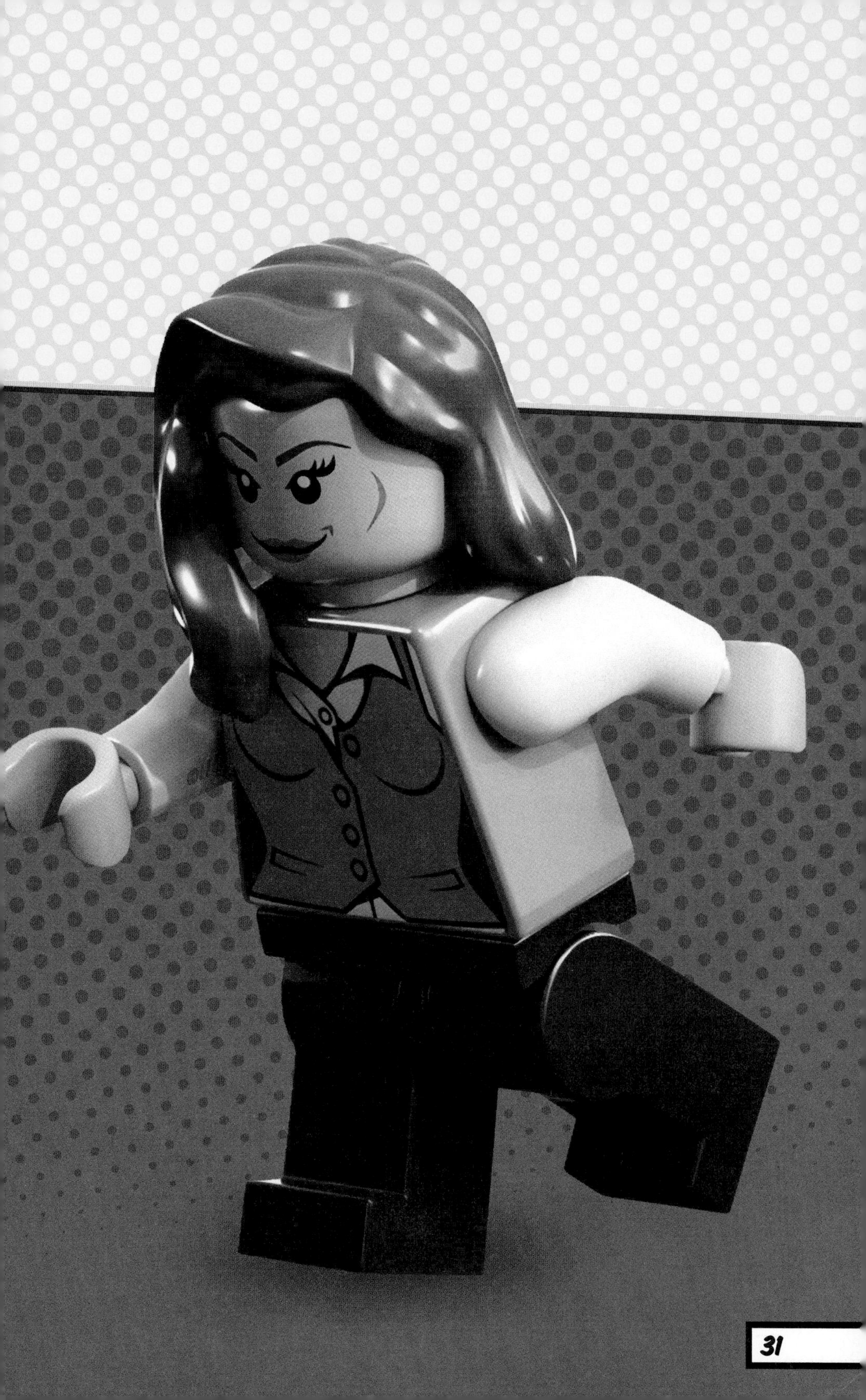

COLONEL HARDY

Colonel Hardy is an important **military officer** whose mission is to stop Kryptonian villains from attacking Earth. Hardy believes that the army should be allowed to fight General Zod and his followers **without help** from super heroes.

EQUIPMENT:
GUN;
MILITARY INTELLIGENCE

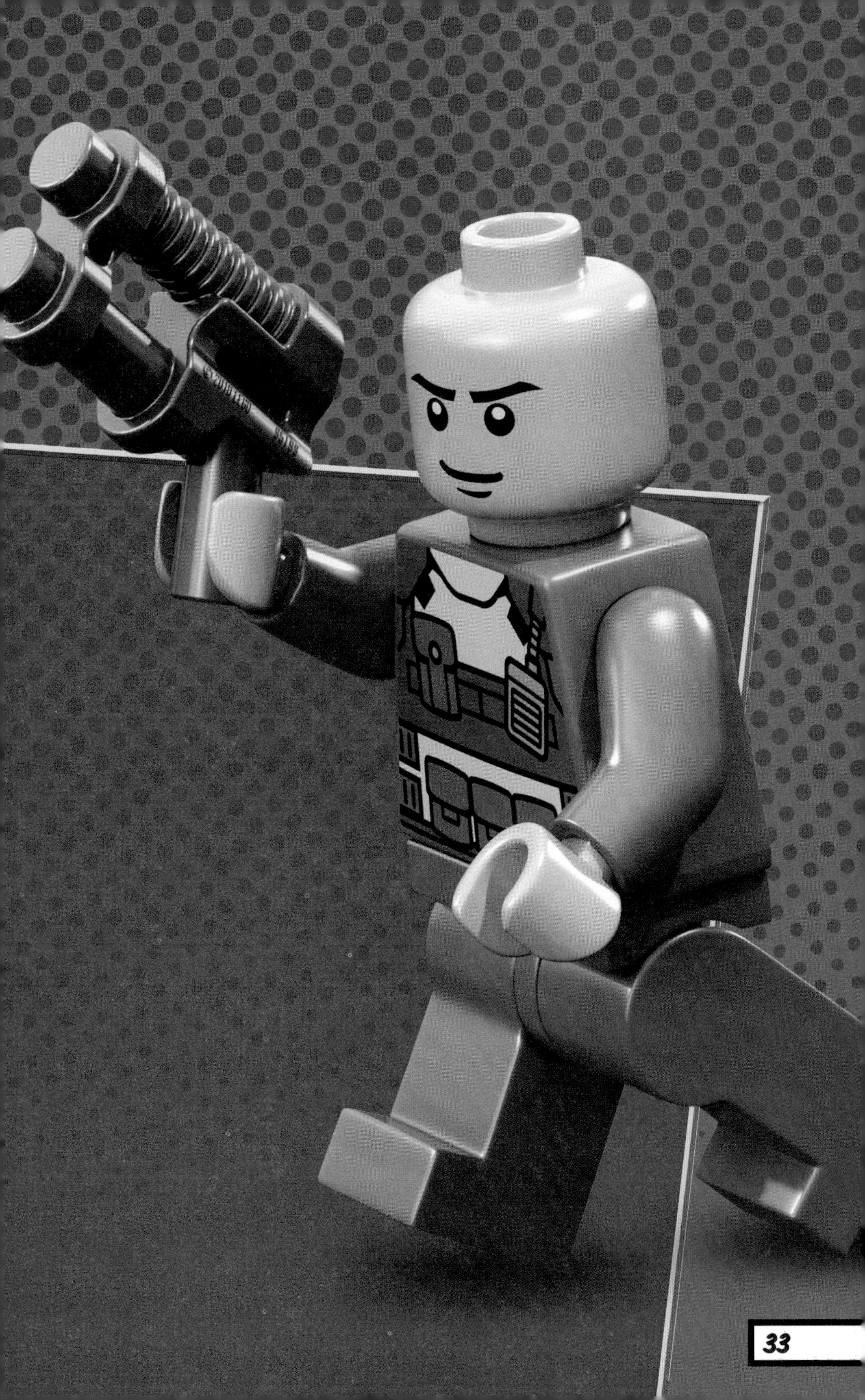

GUARDS

Guards are supposed to **protect** valuable places, like banks, from criminals. Unfortunately, their training doesn't cover super-villains like Two-Face and the Joker. They do their **best**, but they usually need help from the super heroes to save the day.

EQUIPMENT: WALKIE-TALKIES; HANDCUFFS

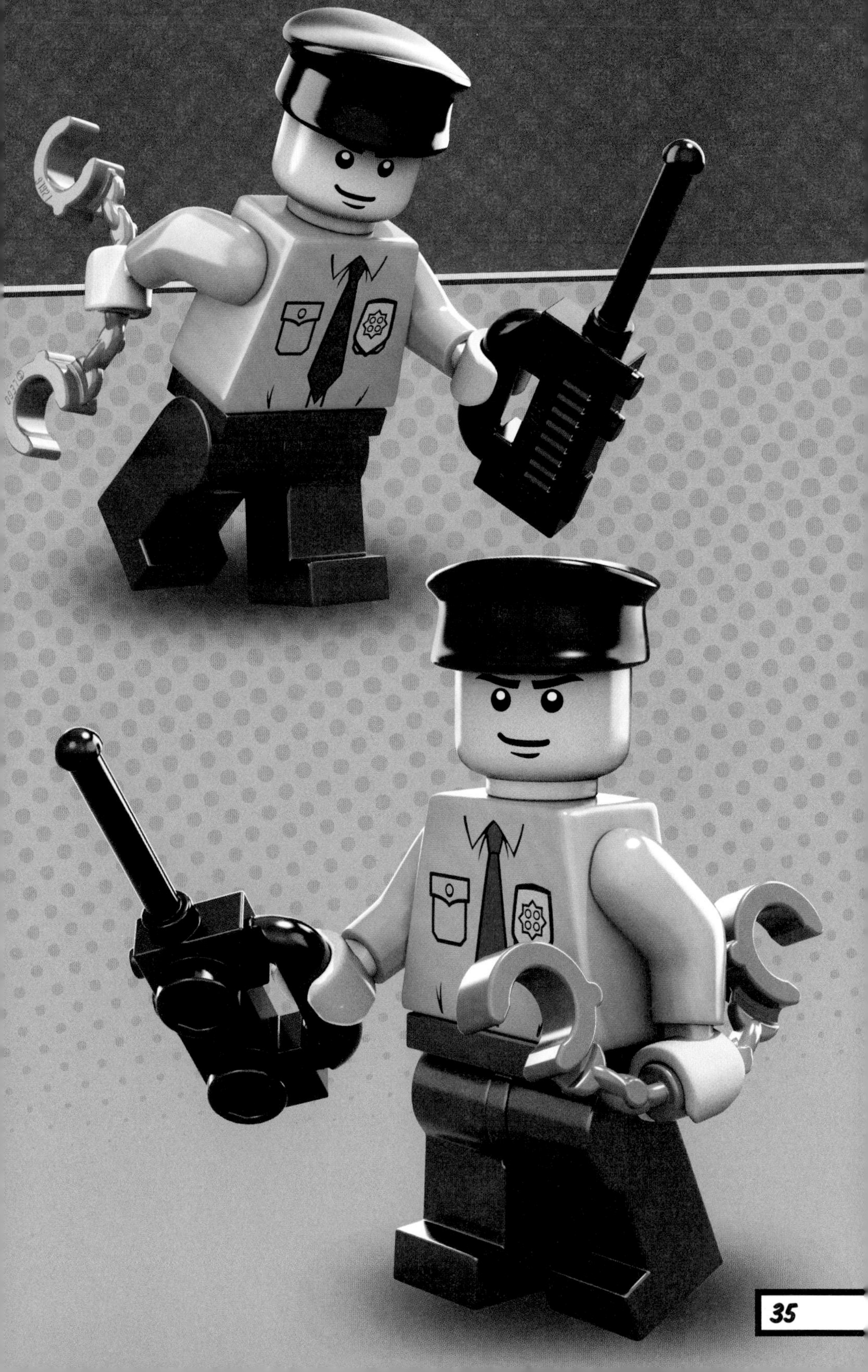

CHAPTER 2

VILLAINS!

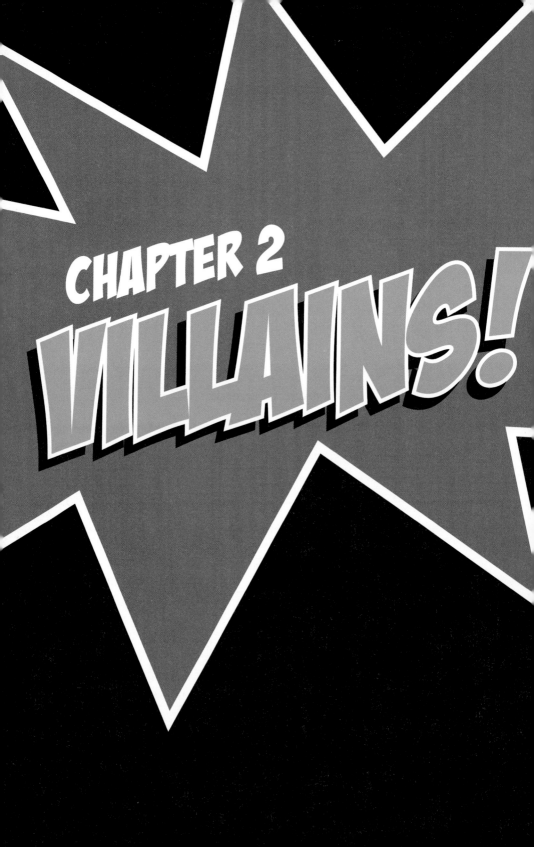

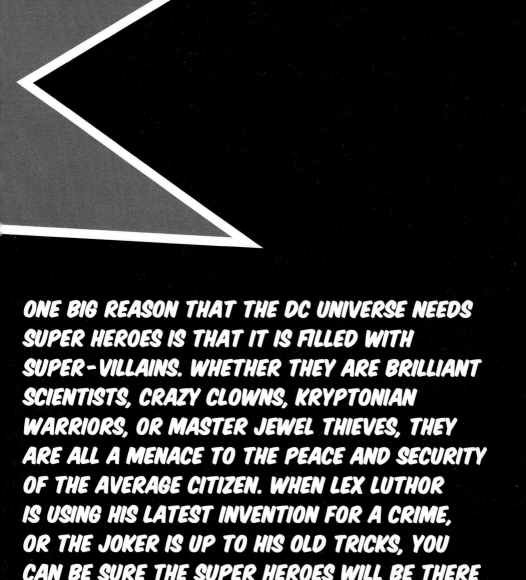

ONE BIG REASON THAT THE DC UNIVERSE NEEDS SUPER HEROES IS THAT IT IS FILLED WITH SUPER-VILLAINS. WHETHER THEY ARE BRILLIANT SCIENTISTS, CRAZY CLOWNS, KRYPTONIAN WARRIORS, OR MASTER JEWEL THIEVES, THEY ARE ALL A MENACE TO THE PEACE AND SECURITY OF THE AVERAGE CITIZEN. WHEN LEX LUTHOR IS USING HIS LATEST INVENTION FOR A CRIME, OR THE JOKER IS UP TO HIS OLD TRICKS, YOU CAN BE SURE THE SUPER HEROES WILL BE THERE TO SHUT THEM DOWN.

LEX LUTHOR

The richest and most powerful man in Metropolis, Luthor knows that only Superman can stop his crooked schemes. He tries everything to defeat the Man of Steel, only to fail again and again. But with his **vast fortune** and **criminal genius**, he never runs out of new inventions to use against the Last Son of Krypton!

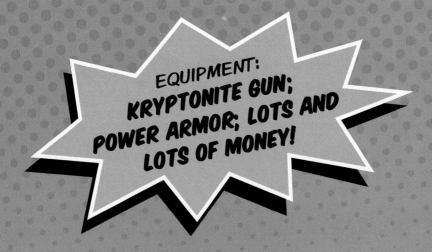

EQUIPMENT:
KRYPTONITE GUN;
POWER ARMOR; LOTS AND
LOTS OF MONEY!

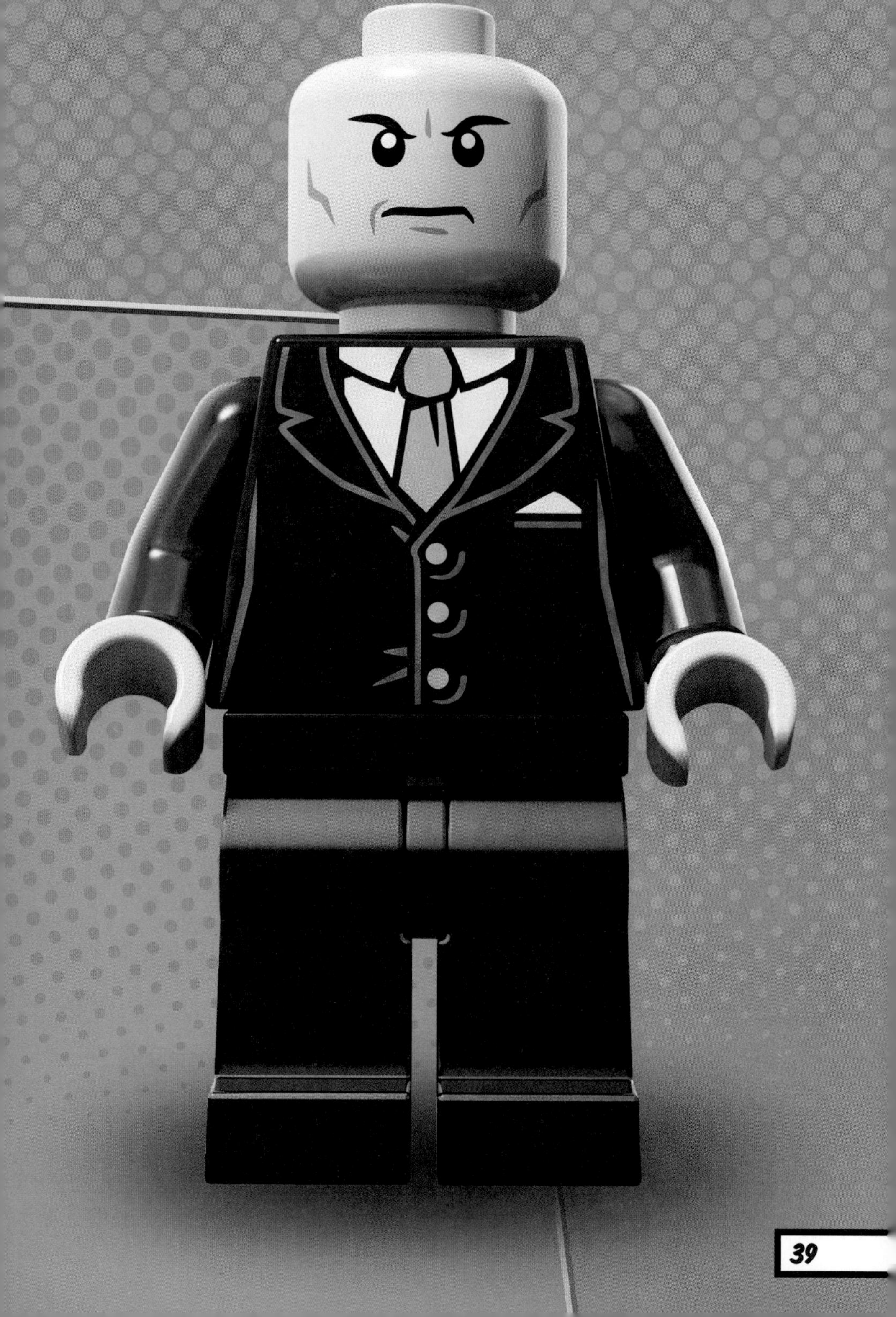

GENERAL ZOD

Zod is a **Kryptonian** military leader who escaped from the **Phantom Zone** and now intends to conquer Earth—or destroy it. Zod is a **master of strategy**, has all the **powers** of Superman, and has other Kryptonian **villains** working with him. He has everything he needs to win—but no one told that to the Man of Steel.

ABILITIES:
FLIGHT, SUPER-STRENGTH, SUPER-SPEED, INVULNERABILITY, X-RAY AND TELESCOPIC VISION, SUPER-HEARING, AND SUPER-BREATH

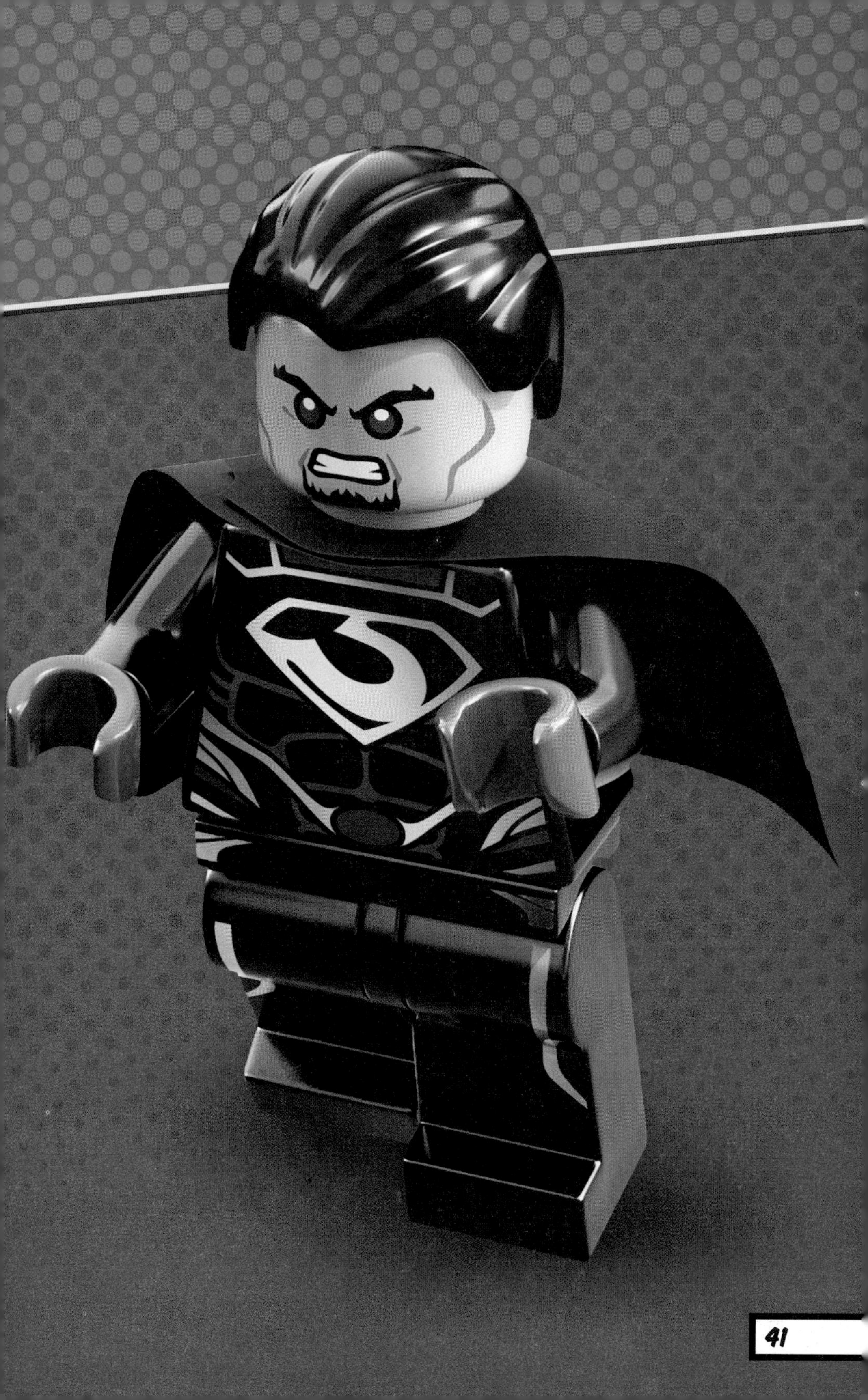

FAORA AND TOR-AN

Faora and Tor-An are two escaped **Kryptonian** criminals under the leadership of General Zod. They are ready to pit their incredible powers against Superman in a struggle for the fate of Earth. **Ruthless** and **highly dangerous**, they are two of the most powerful opponents Superman has ever faced.

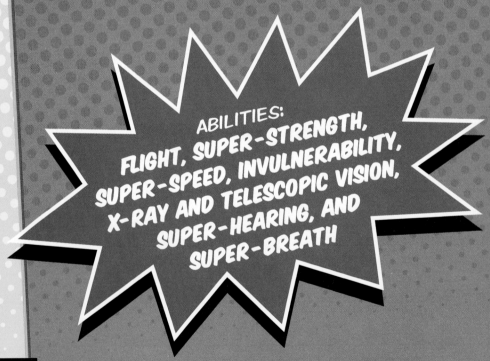

ABILITIES:
FLIGHT, SUPER-STRENGTH, SUPER-SPEED, INVULNERABILITY, X-RAY AND TELESCOPIC VISION, SUPER-HEARING, AND SUPER-BREATH

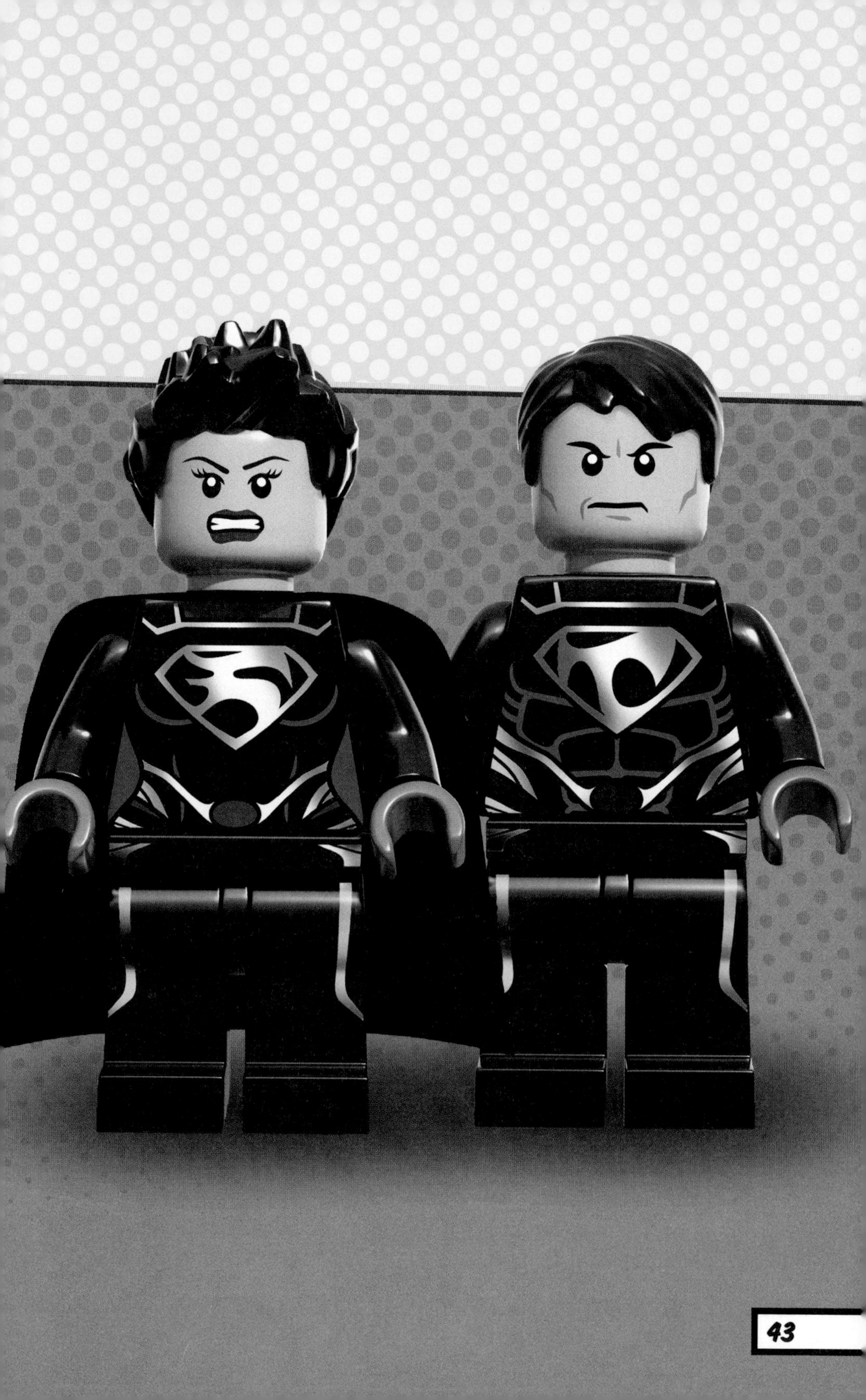

THE JOKER

The Joker's crimes almost always involve jokes (usually bad ones) and his dangerous **Joker toxin**. Batman always spoils his plans and they have become archenemies over the years. Sometimes it seems that the Joker commits crimes just so he can fight with Batman again. When he is not on the loose in Gotham City, the Joker spends his time locked up at **Arkham Asylum**.

REAL NAME:
UNKNOWN

EQUIPMENT:
**"BANG" FLAG SPEAR GUN;
ELECTRIC JOY BUZZER;
JOKER TOXIN**

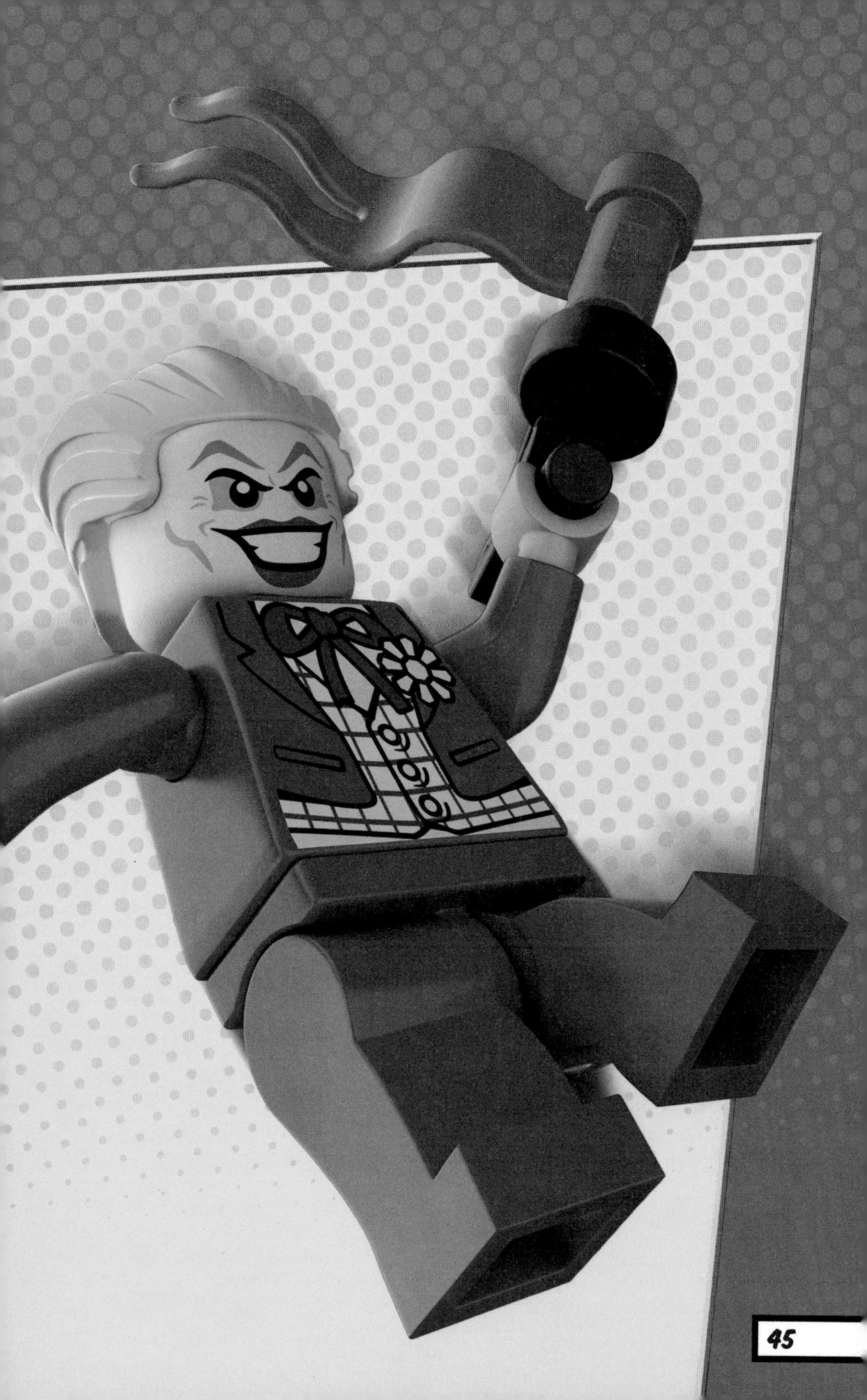

HARLEY QUINN

Harleen Quinzel was once the Joker's doctor at **Arkham Asylum**. The Joker told her lies about himself, and she fell in love with him. After helping him escape from the asylum, she put on a costume and became his **sidekick**, Harley Quinn. She is a great acrobat and a skilled burglar.

REAL NAME:
DR. HARLEEN QUINZEL

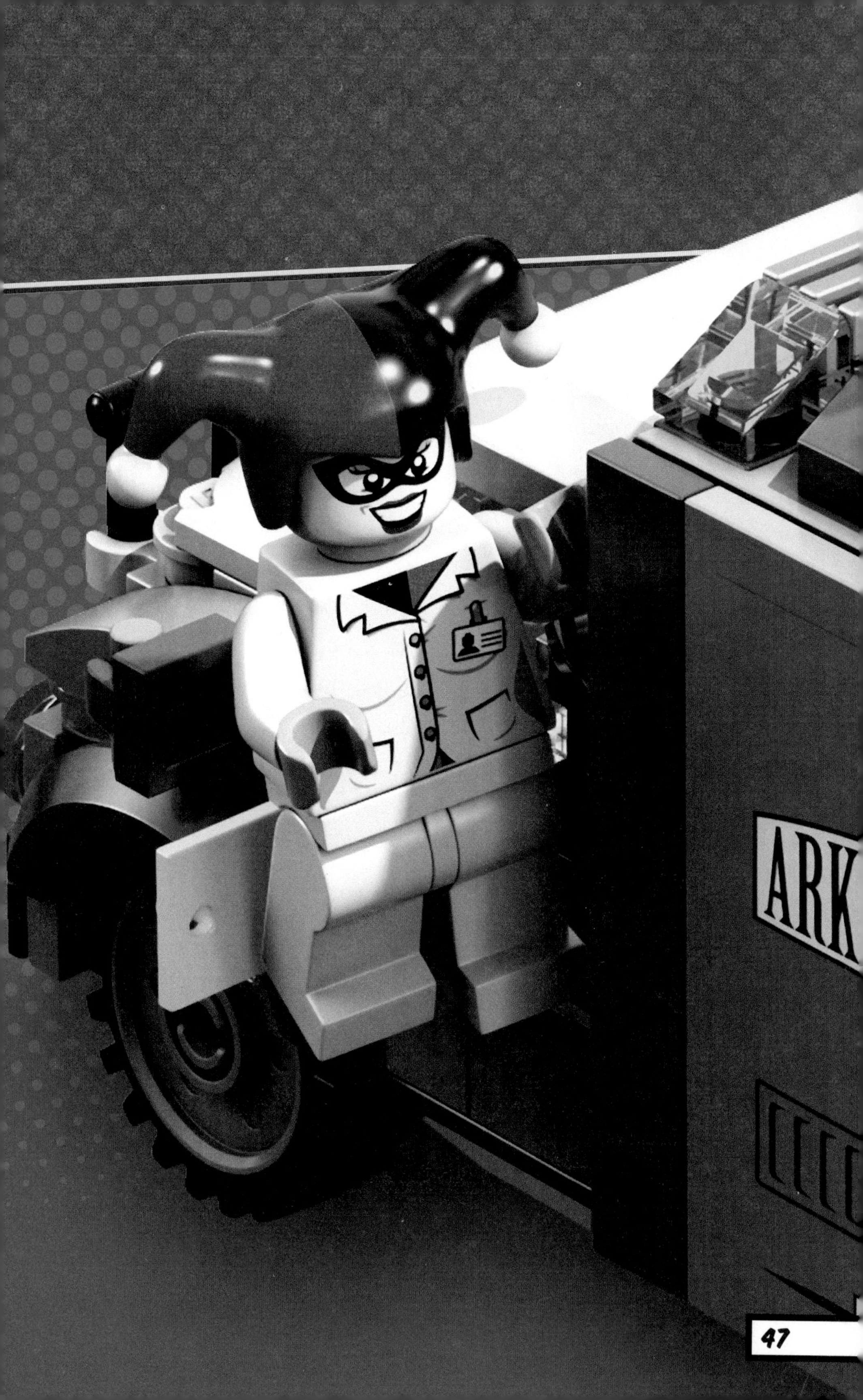
ARK

BANE

Bane is a criminal who wants to take over Gotham City's underworld. Knowing that the people of **Gotham City** look up to Batman, he decides that he must first defeat the Dark Knight to prove his power. To do this, Bane has tried attacking Batman on his own and teamed up with other villains. Although he has given Batman many hard fights, the Dark Knight always wins in the end.

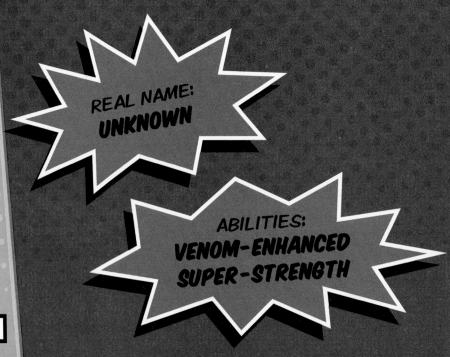

REAL NAME:
UNKNOWN

ABILITIES:
**VENOM-ENHANCED
SUPER-STRENGTH**

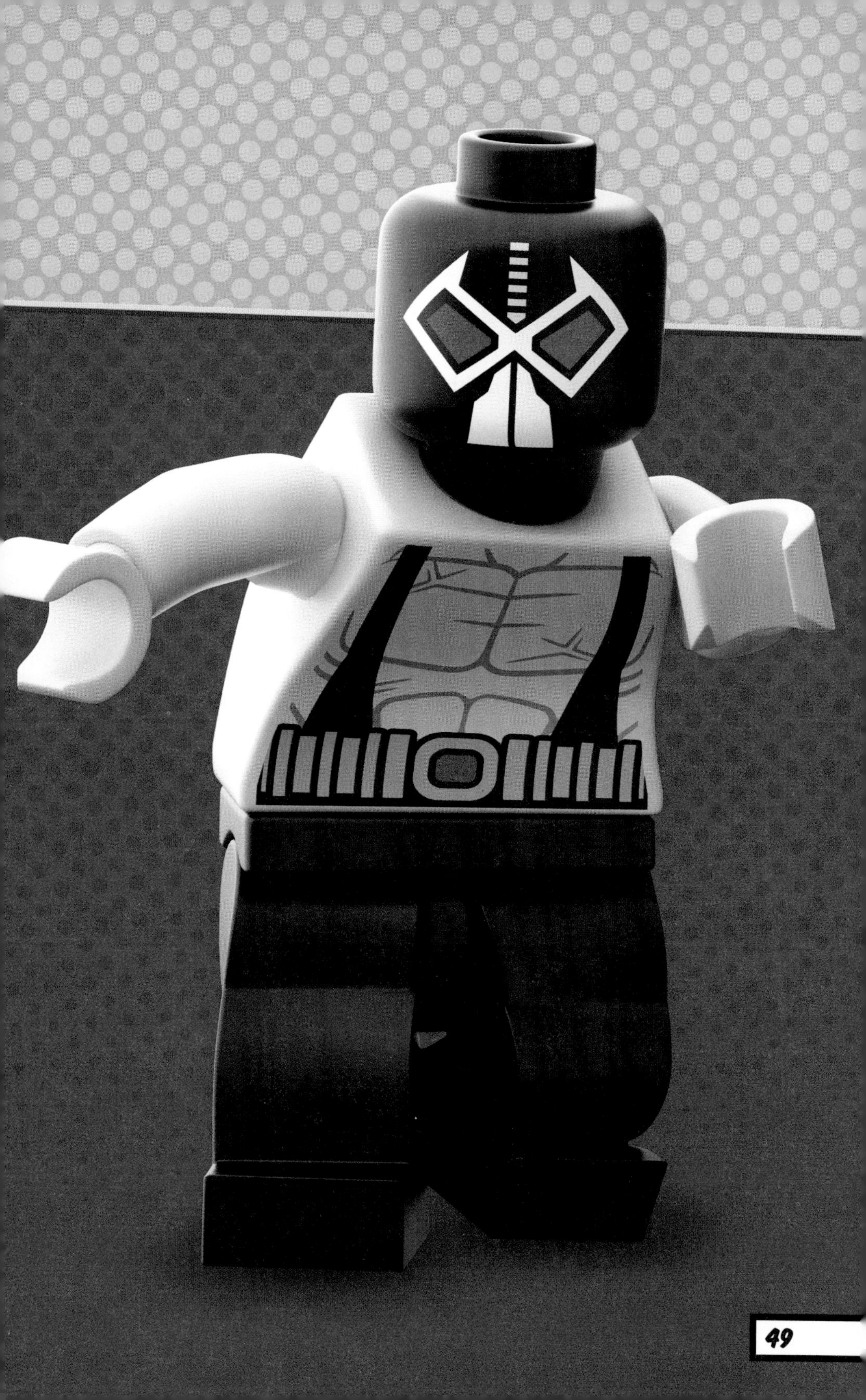

CATWOMAN

Catwoman is a highly skilled thief. Her acrobatics and **martial arts skills** have always made her a challenge for Batman. Although they are often on opposite sides of the law, Catwoman has **helped** Batman more than once when **Gotham City** was in danger. In return, Batman has sometimes let her "escape" rather than turn her over to the police.

REAL NAME:
SELINA KYLE

EQUIPMENT:
WHIP; CAT CLAWS

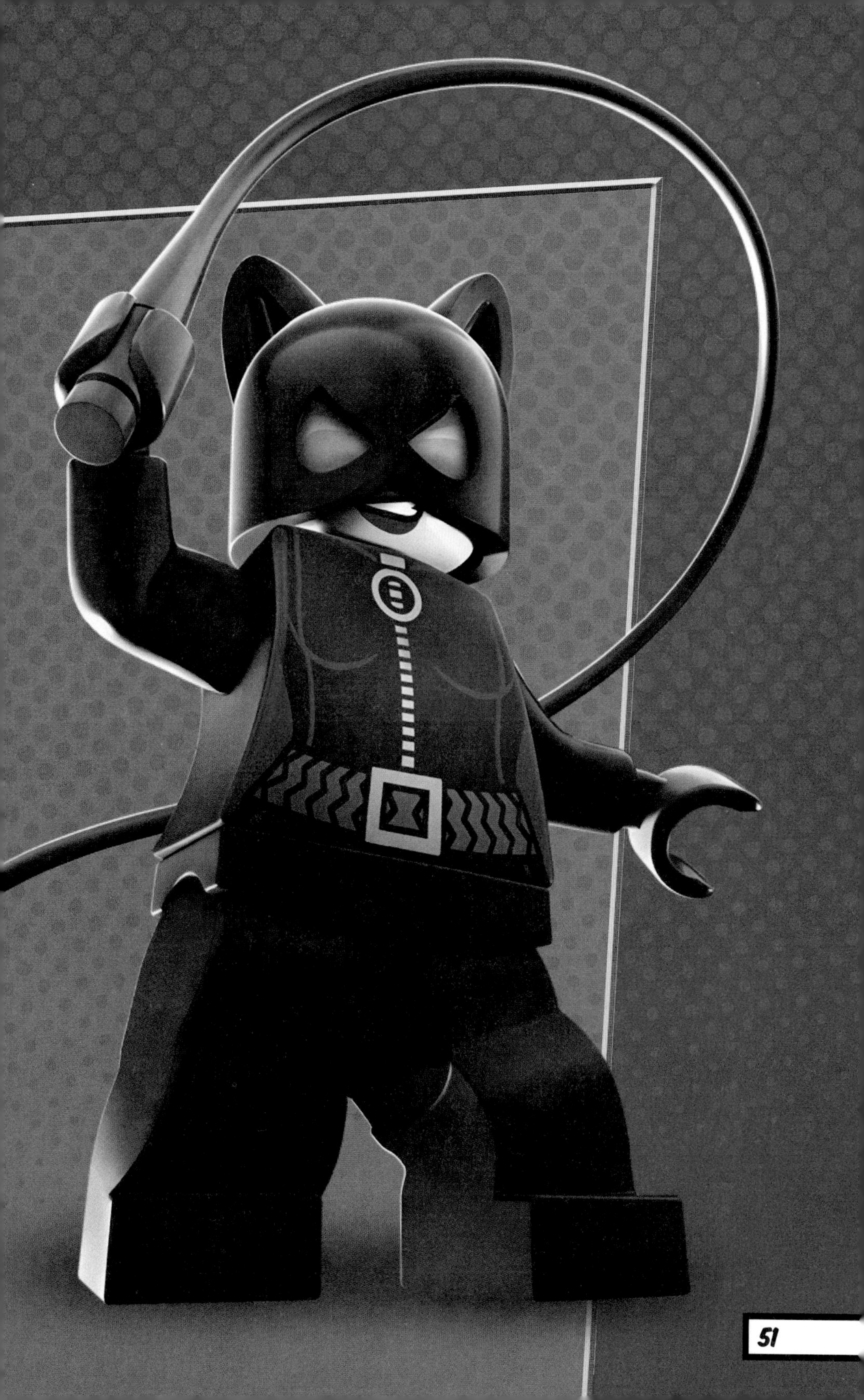

TWO-FACE

Harvey Dent was **Gotham City**'s district attorney. Then a terrible accident resulted in half his face being scarred. Calling himself Two-Face, he became a crook, basing all of his crimes on the **number two**. Before each crime, Two-Face flips his two-headed coin, one side of which is **scarred**. He uses the coin to make all his important decisions, which makes him **unpredictable**.

REAL NAME:
HARVEY DENT

EQUIPMENT:
GUNS; TWO-HEADED COIN

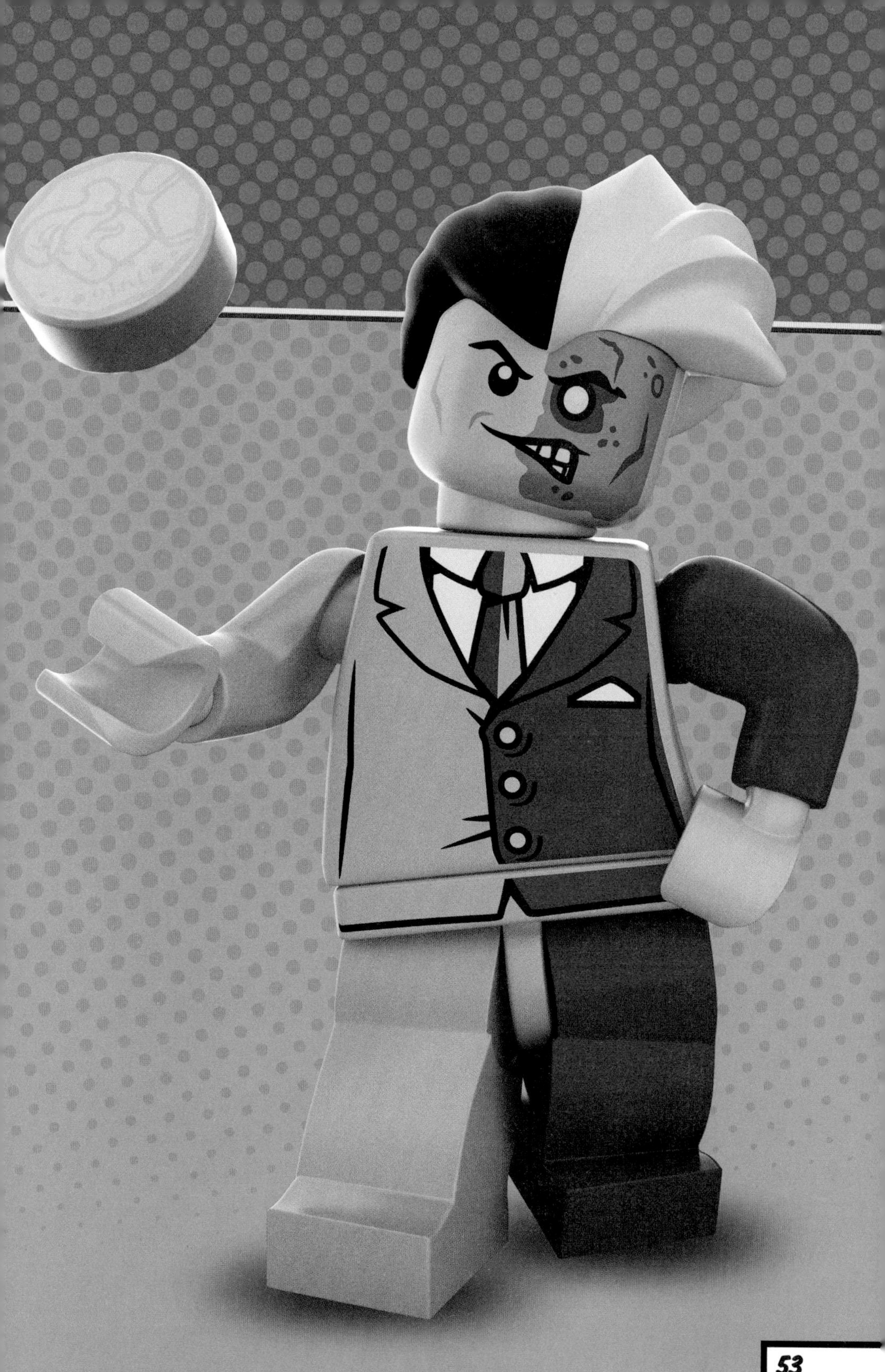

POISON IVY

Pamela Isley was an expert on flowers and other plants before a freak accident in her lab turned her into Poison Ivy. Now she can **control plants**, **poison** others with her kiss, and even create new creatures that are half-human, half-tree. Poison Ivy uses robbery and blackmail to make money. Although she is not skilled in battle, she is clever, cunning, and very good at setting **traps** for the heroes.

REAL NAME:
PAMELA ISLEY

ABILITIES:
SHE IS CAPABLE OF CONTROLLING MANY TYPES OF PLANTS.

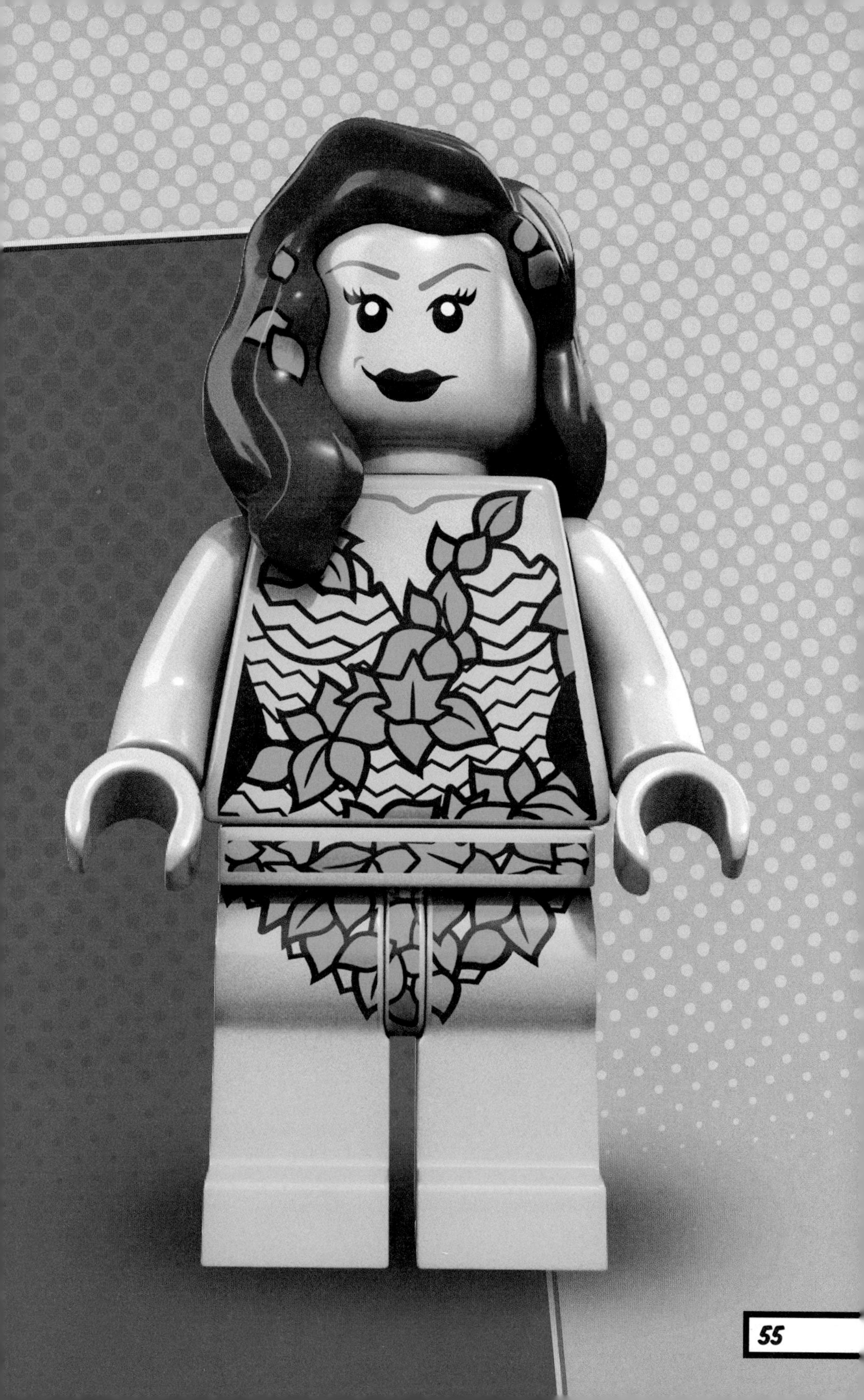

THE RIDDLER

The Riddler loves puzzles. He uses his skill at coming up with **riddles** to challenge Batman and the police. Before every crime, the Riddler leaves a riddle clue for Batman. In fact, he can't commit a robbery without giving Batman a **clue** first! Although he usually works alone, the Riddler has teamed up with the Joker in the past and sometimes has a gang of his own.

REAL NAME:
EDWARD NIGMA

EQUIPMENT:
CROWBAR; SOMETIMES USES WEAPONS IN THE SHAPE OF QUESTION MARKS

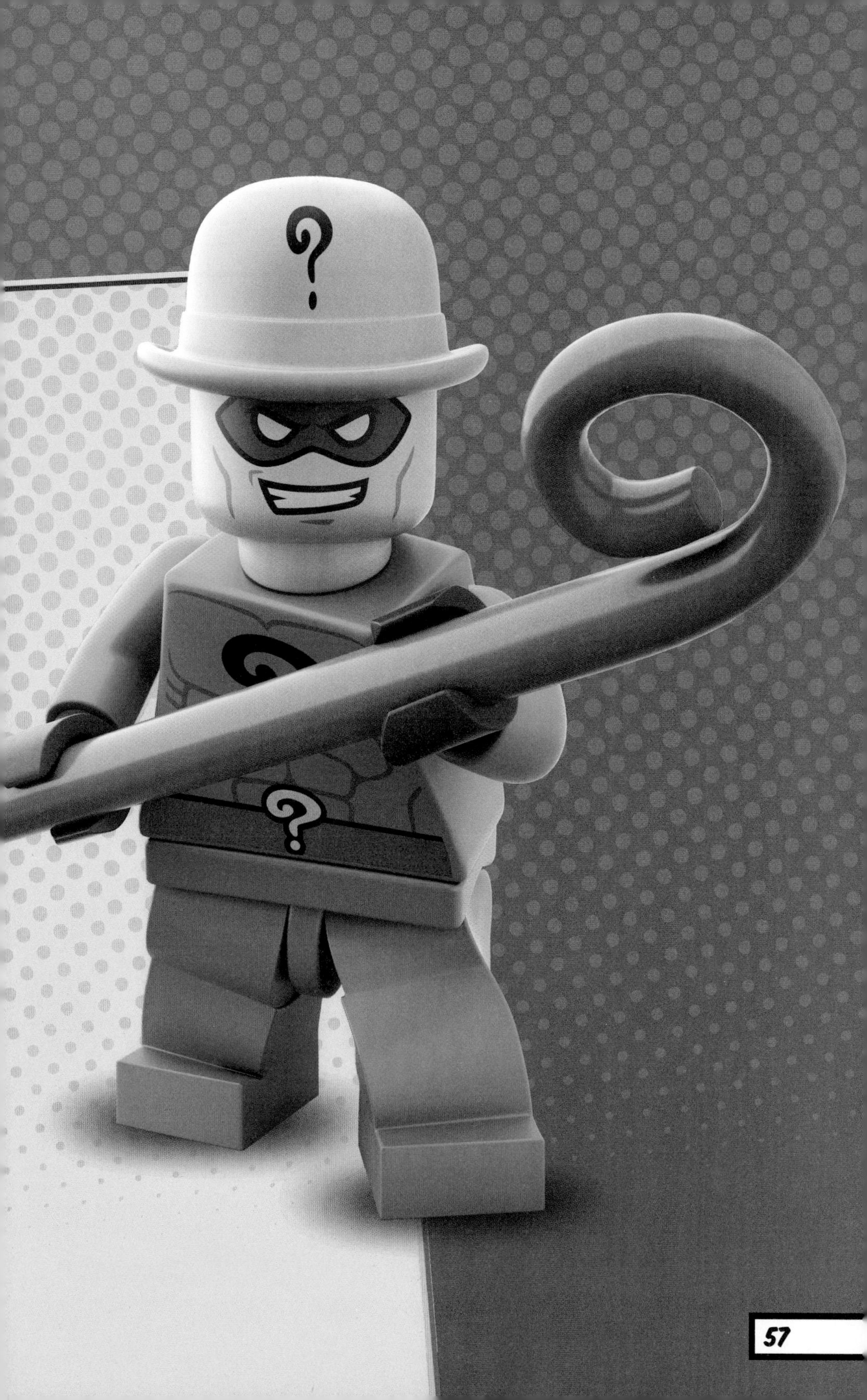

SCARECROW

The Scarecrow uses a **fear toxin** he invented to frighten people just for fun! In his many fights with Batman, he has tried again and again to scare the Dark Knight into a defeat. But Batman is smart enough to know that there is nothing to be afraid of, and brave enough not to let the Scarecrow win.

REAL NAME:
JONATHAN CRANE

EQUIPMENT:
FEAR TOXIN

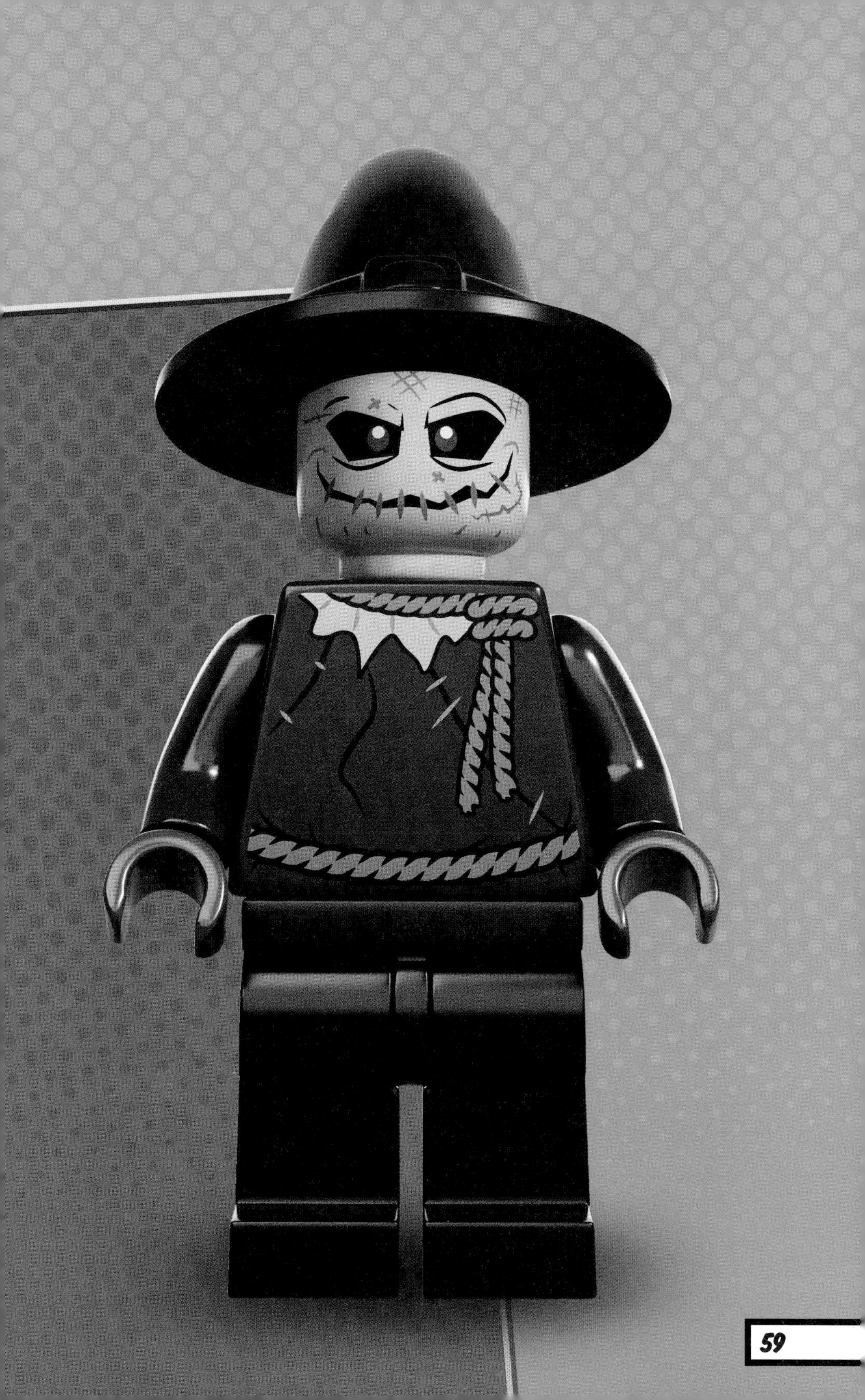

MR. FREEZE

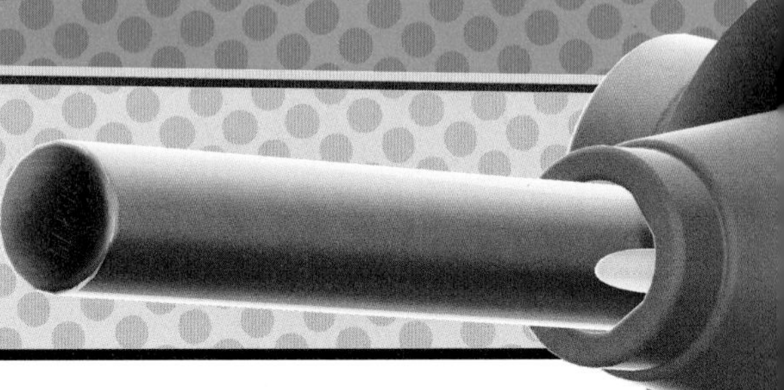

The man who became the icy villain Mr. Freeze was once a scientist studying the use of extreme cold to preserve people until the cures for their illnesses could be found. A lab accident changed him so that he could only exist in **sub-zero temperatures**. Wearing **armor** that both increases his strength and keeps him ice-cold, Mr. Freeze commits **jewel thefts** to fund his research.

REAL NAME:
VICTOR FRIES

EQUIPMENT:
FREEZE GUN

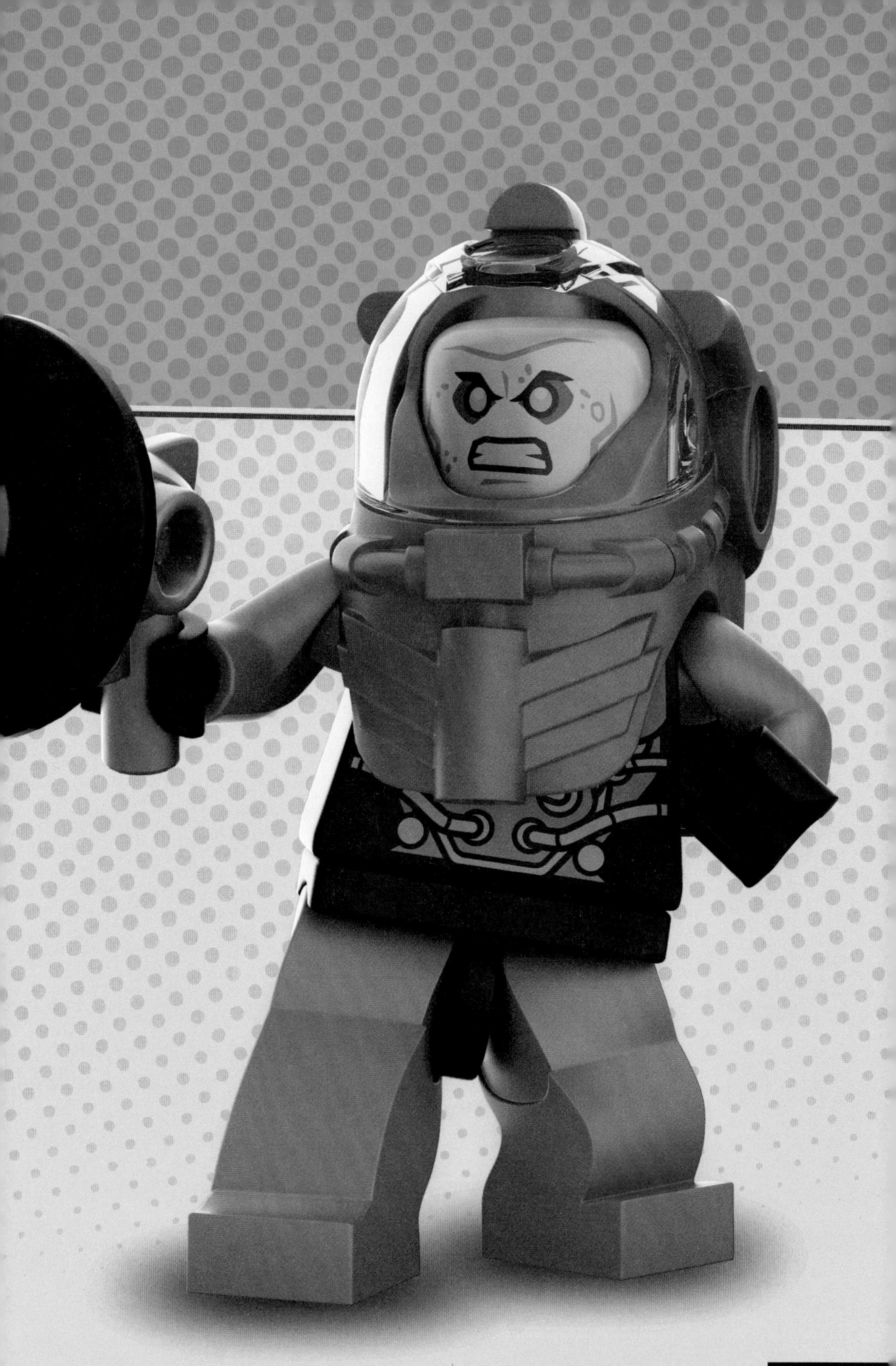

THE PENGUIN

The Penguin is a master criminal whose crimes always have something to do with birds. His favorite weapon is the **umbrella**, and he has hundreds of different kinds. These include umbrellas that allow him to **fly**, umbrellas that **shoot fire** or **poison gas**, and even **bulletproof** umbrellas he can use as a shield.

REAL NAME:
OSWALD COBBLEPOT

EQUIPMENT:
A VARIETY OF TRICK UMBRELLAS

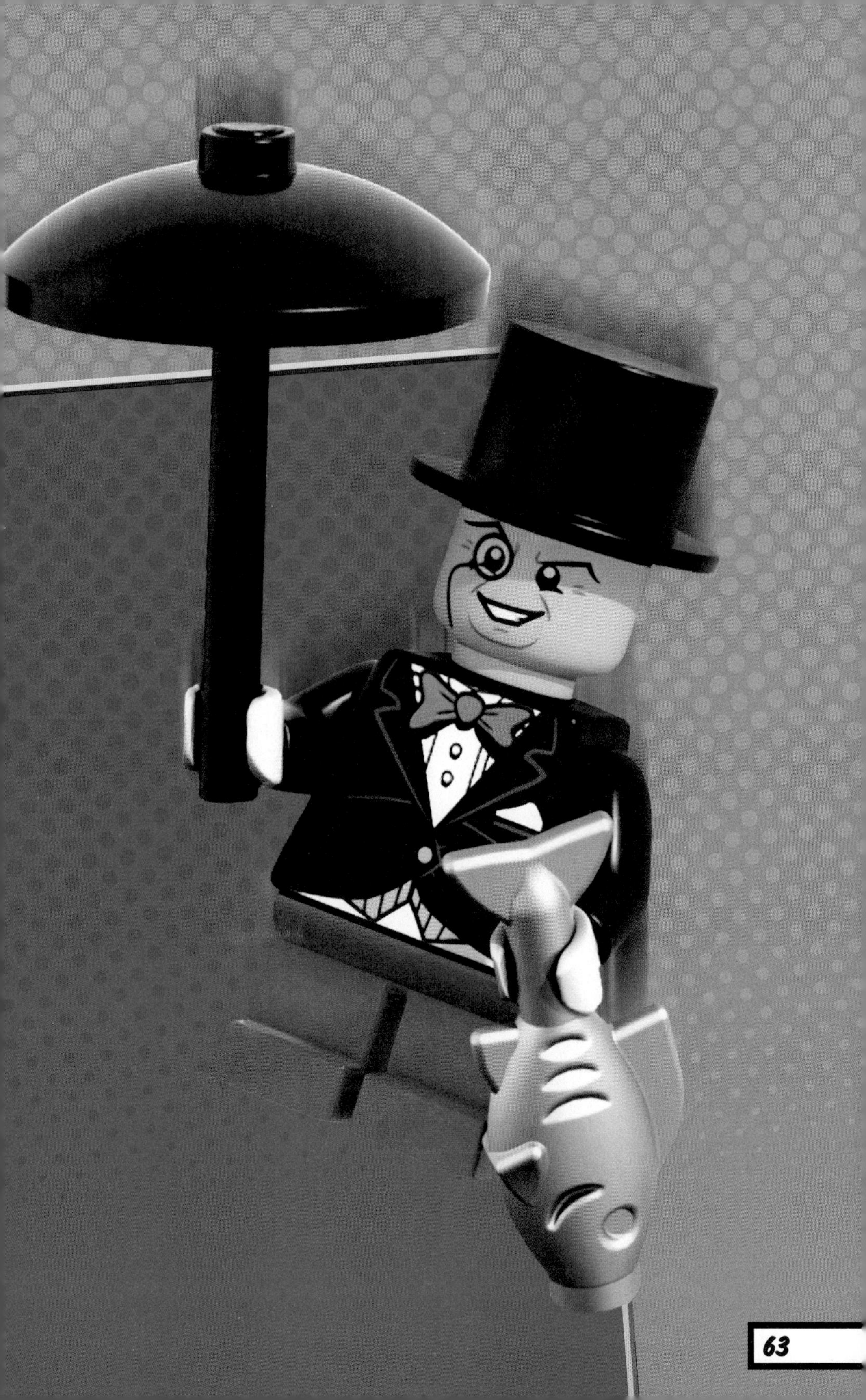

HENCHMEN

Most super-villains have henchmen. They **help** with the heavy lifting during crimes, **guard the hideout**, and do other jobs someone like the Joker or the Penguin can't be bothered with. Henchmen tend to not be very bright, but there are usually a lot of them and they can keep a super hero **busy** for maybe a couple of minutes in a fight.

EQUIPMENT:
CROWBARS,
WALKIE-TALKIES

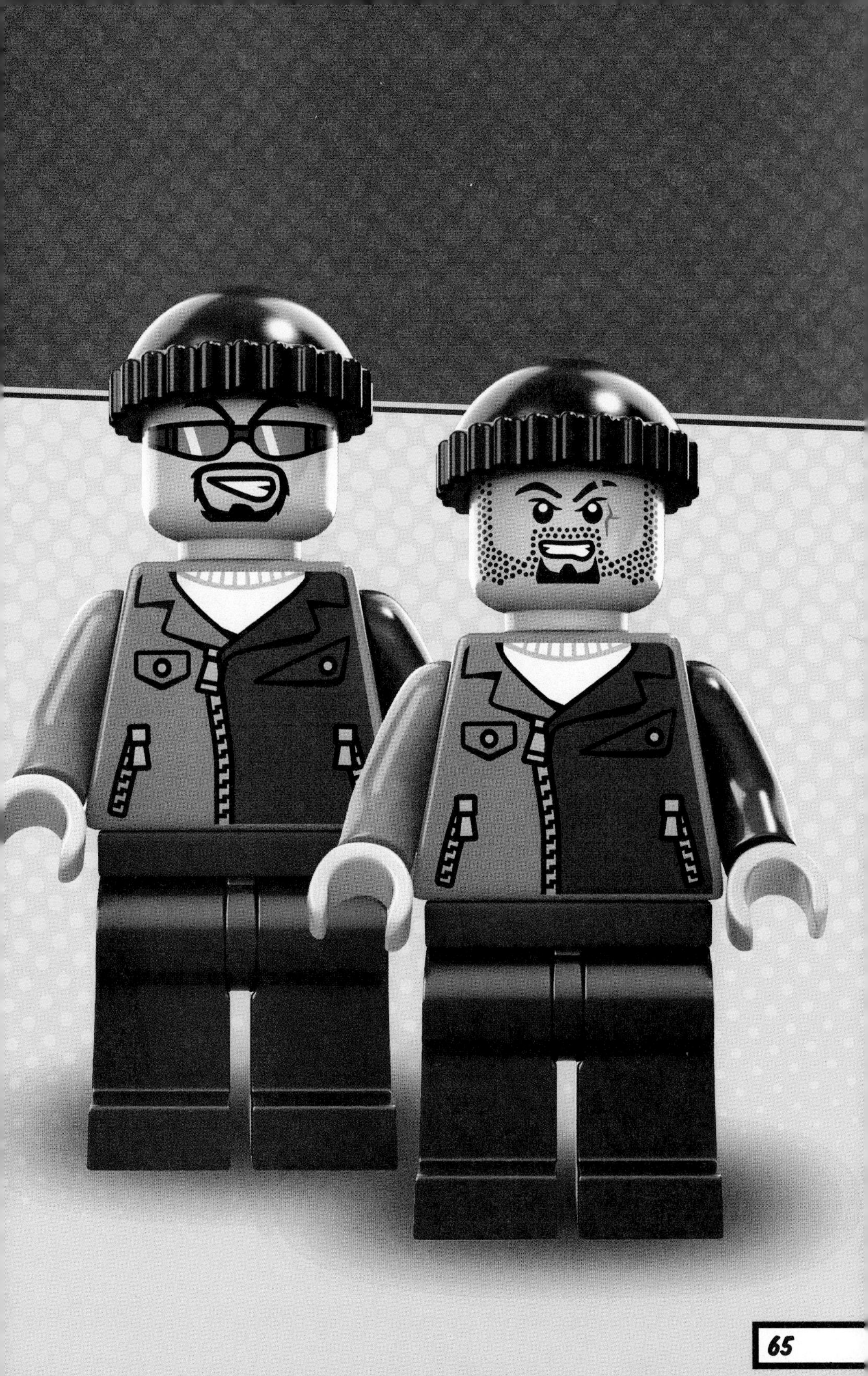

A SUPER HERO CANNOT STOP A CRIME UNLESS HE CAN GET TO IT IN TIME, AND A SUPER-VILLAIN CANNOT HOPE TO MAKE A GETAWAY IF HE DOESN'T HAVE SOME WAY TO GET FROM PLACE TO PLACE. OUR FAVORITE HEROES AND VILLAINS HAVE ALL KINDS OF AWESOME RIDES—INCLUDING CARS, BOATS, PLANES, AND EVEN SPACECRAFT!

CHAPTER 3
VEHICLES!

THE BATMOBILE

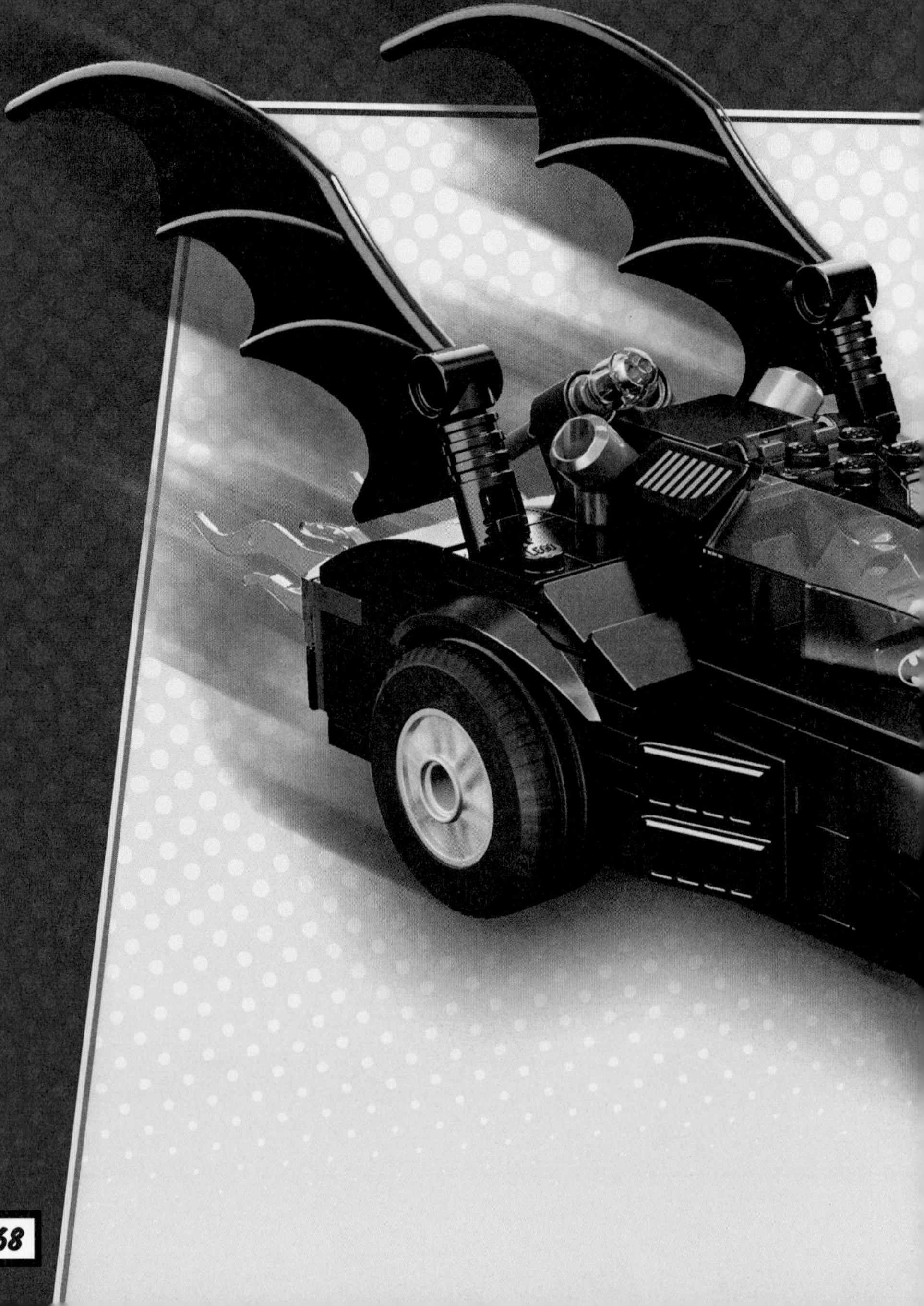

One of the fastest cars in the world, the Batmobile is a vital tool in Batman's war on criminals. It features **dual missiles** on the front, plus **special armor** that allows pieces to fly off the car if it is struck rather than toward the passengers. Inside, the Batmobile's computer is linked to the mainframes in the Batcave. There is also a **police scanner**, **automatic pilot**, and more, plus controls to allow Batman to direct the car remotely by voice commands.

THE BATWING

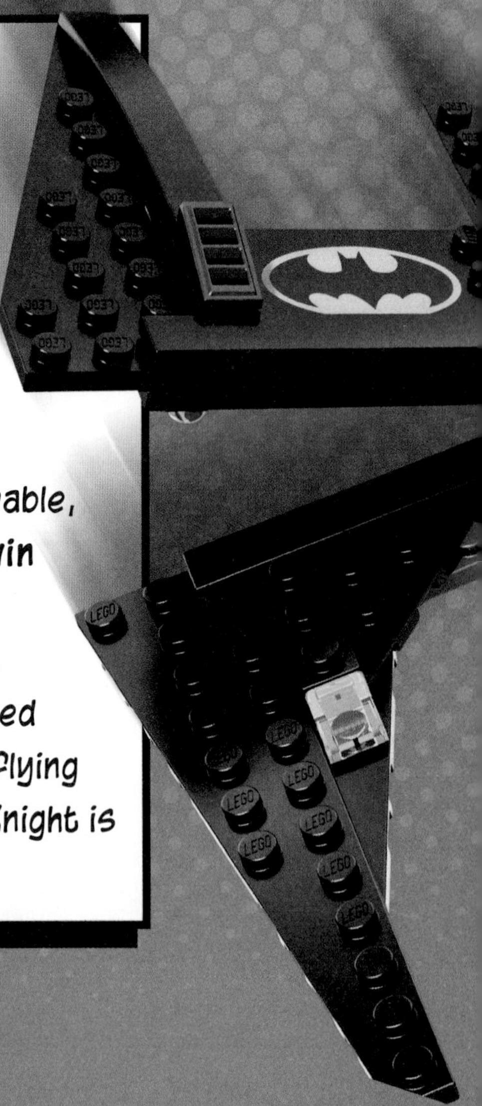

Sometimes, the fight against crime means Batman has to take to the air. The Batwing is the latest in a long line of aircraft Batman has used to battle Gotham City's villains. In addition to being incredibly fast and maneuverable, the Batwing is armed with **twin air-to-air missiles** and is completely invisible to radar. Its engine is specially designed to make almost **no noise**, so flying villains won't know the Dark Knight is coming for them.

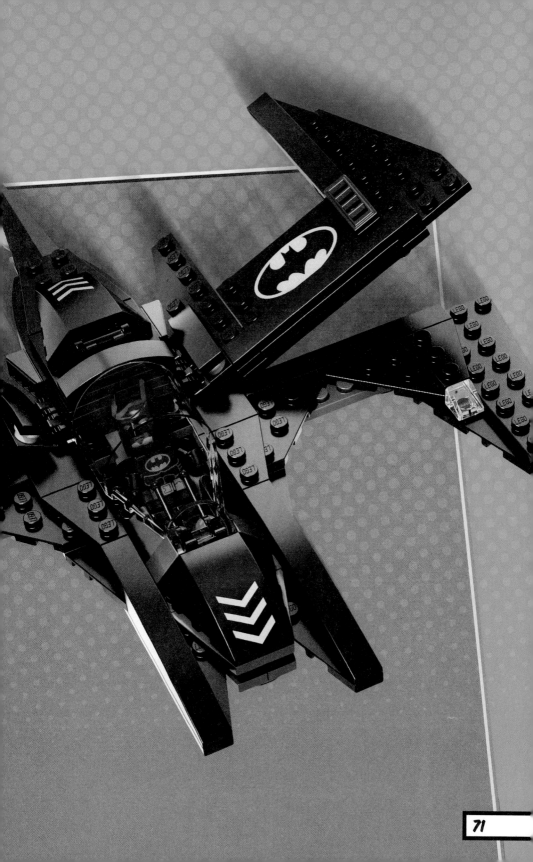

THE BATBOAT

When criminals strike on the water, Batman races to the scene in his Batboat. This watercraft features a **radar/sonar array** in the nose, an **armored hull**, **a jet engine**, and **twin surface-to-surface missiles**. The Batboat is kept docked in Sublevel 6 of the Batcave, ready to be launched via underground tunnel into the Gotham River or Gotham Bay.

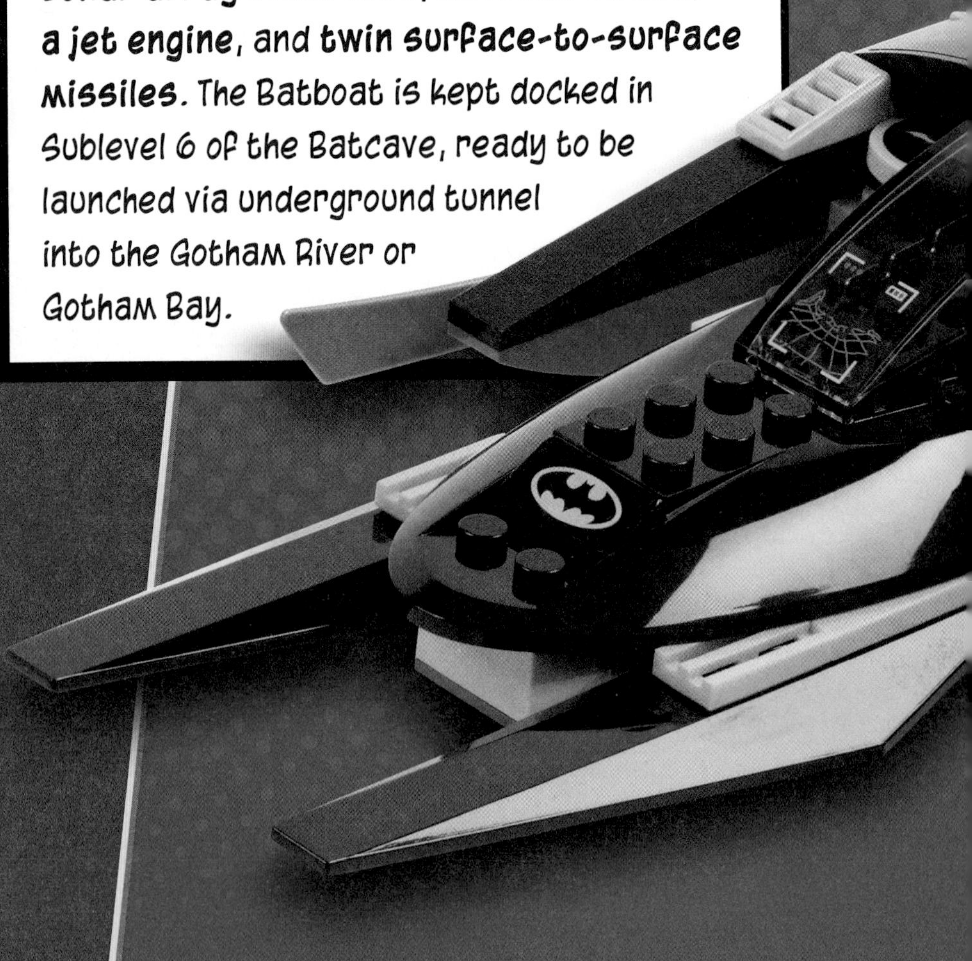

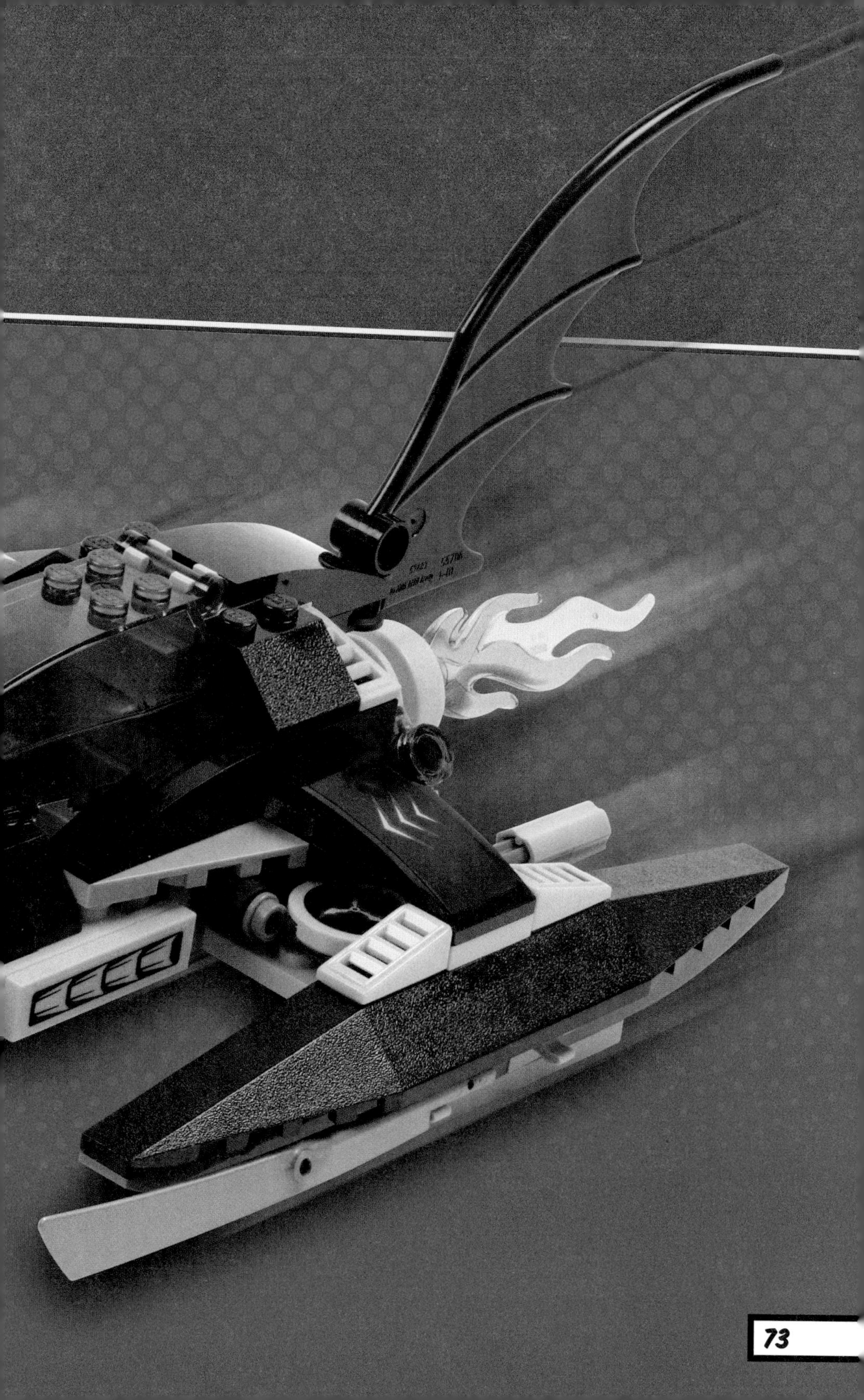

THE BATCYCLE

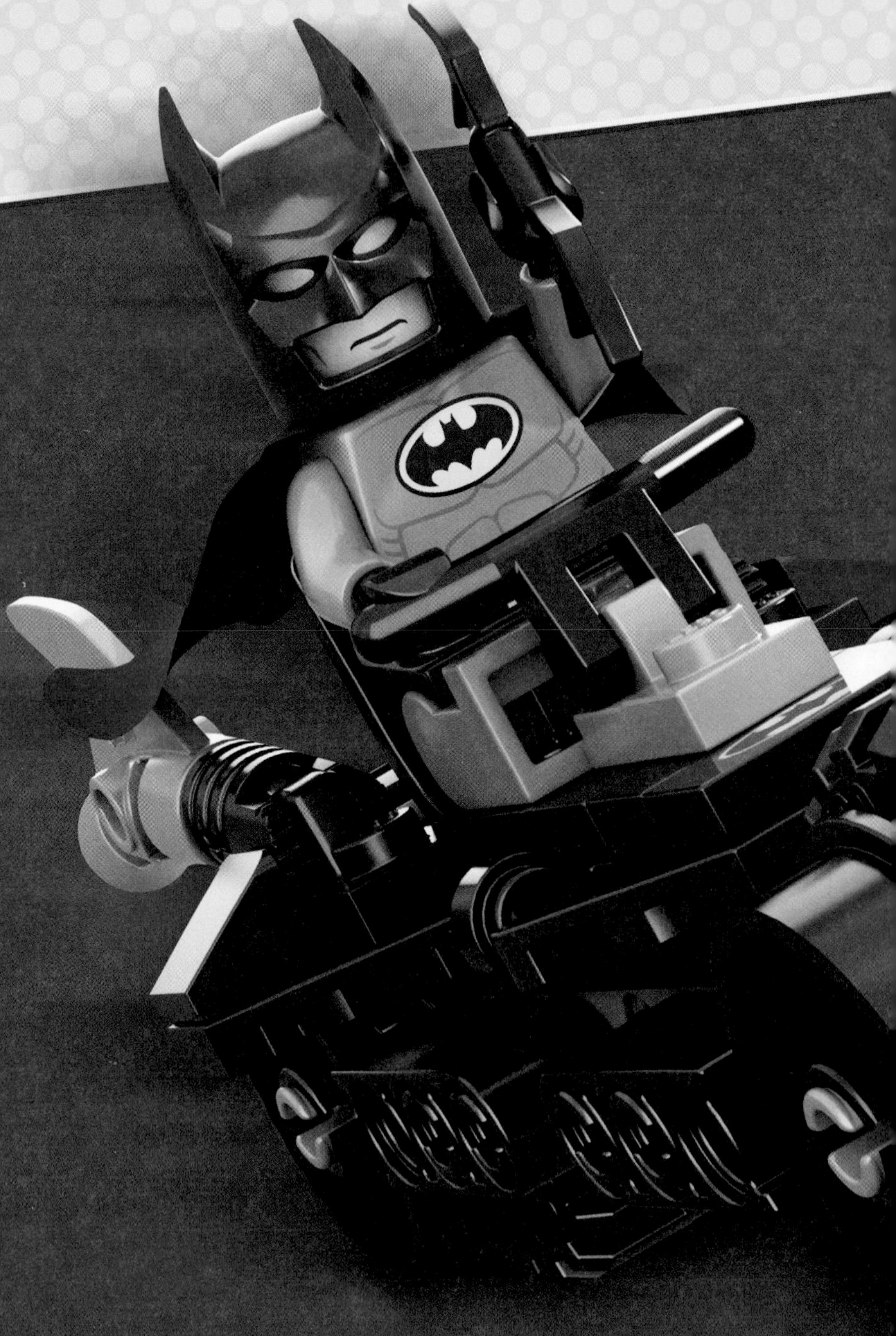

On missions where the Batmobile would be too easily spotted, Batman relies on his Batcycle. Batman has a number of **different models** of Batcycle, including some that can be taken apart and stored in the trunk of the Batmobile for **easy transport.**

THE BAT

There isn't always time or room to take off in the Batwing. That's when Batman uses the Bat, a **jump jet** designed by Wayne Enterprises capable of **vertical takeoffs and landings**. The Bat can fly through narrow alleyways, is armed with **twin guns**, and is outfitted with an **automatic pilot**. Batman uses the Bat to battle Bane in Gotham City.

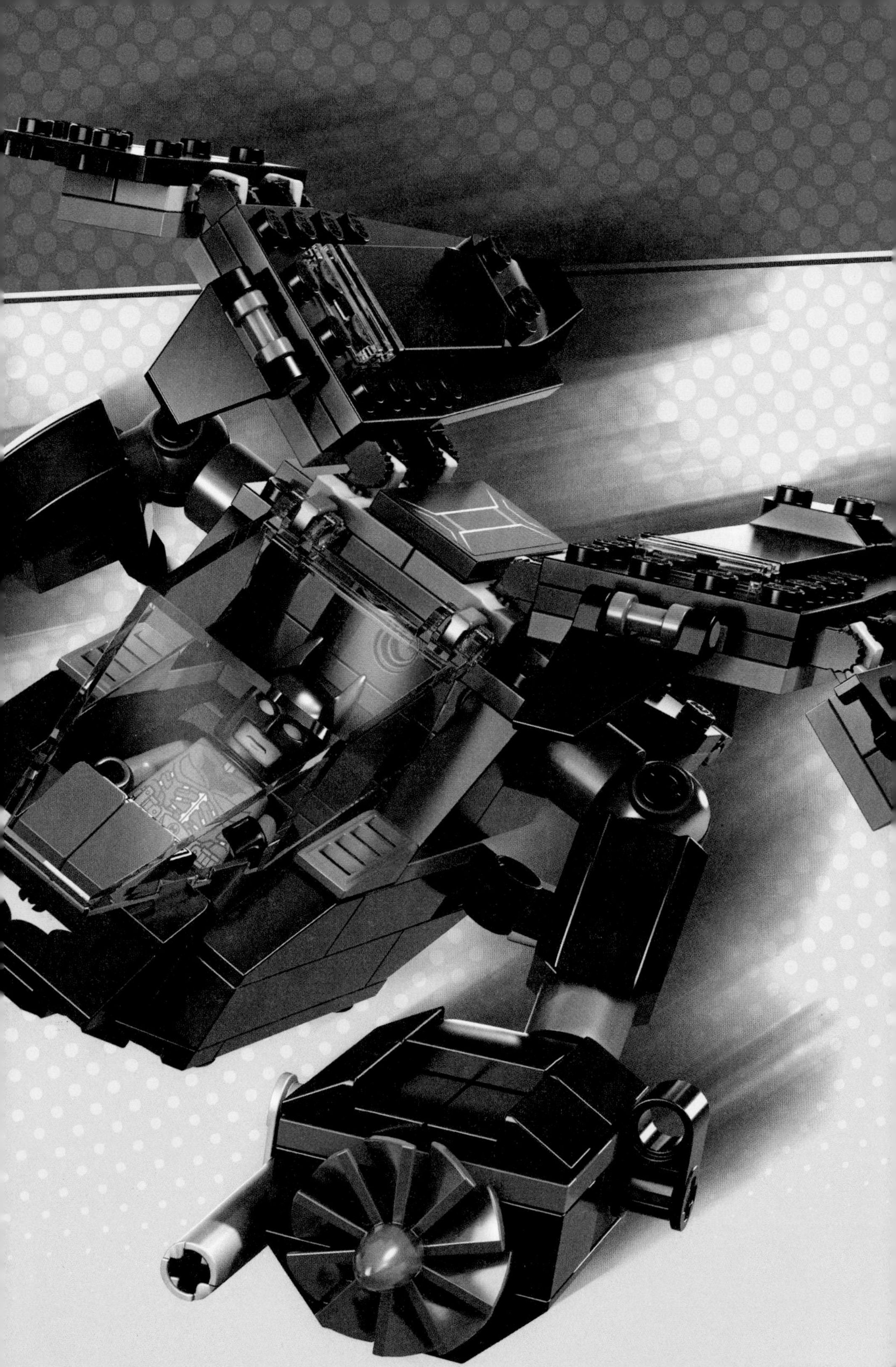

THE JOKER'S HELICOPTER

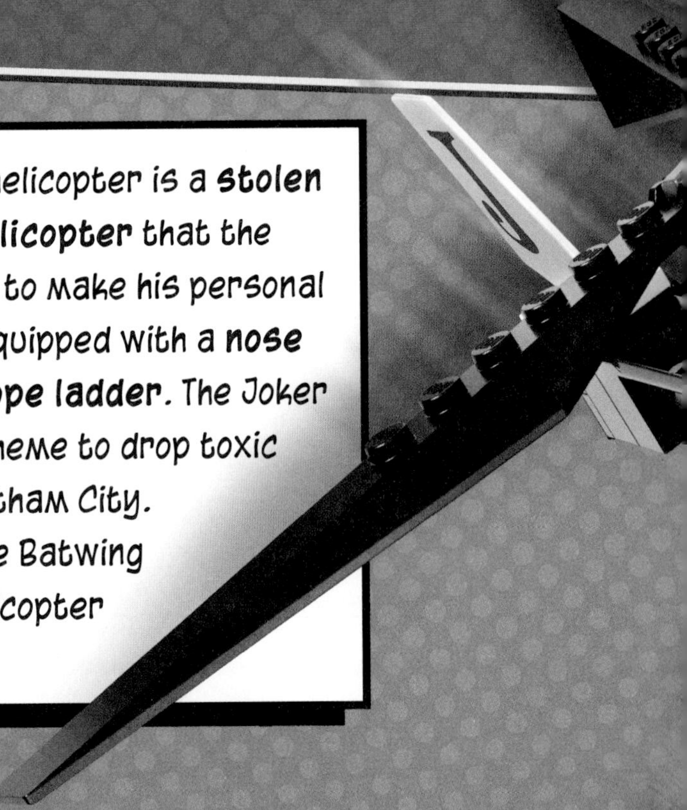

The Joker's helicopter is a **stolen military helicopter** that the Joker repainted to make his personal aircraft. It is equipped with a **nose missile** and a **rope ladder**. The Joker used it in his scheme to drop toxic Joker gas on Gotham City. Batman used the Batwing to knock the helicopter out of the sky.

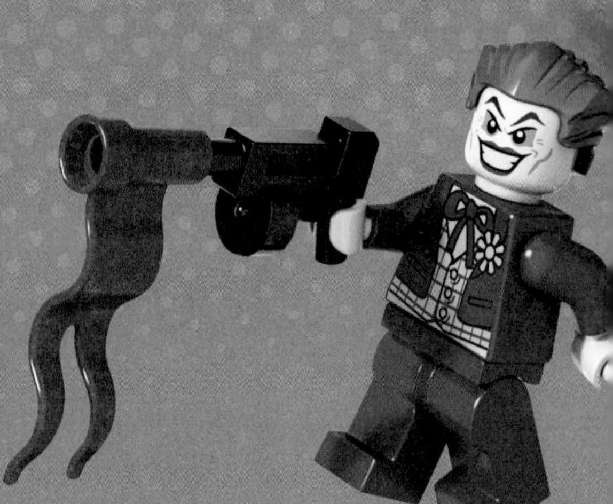

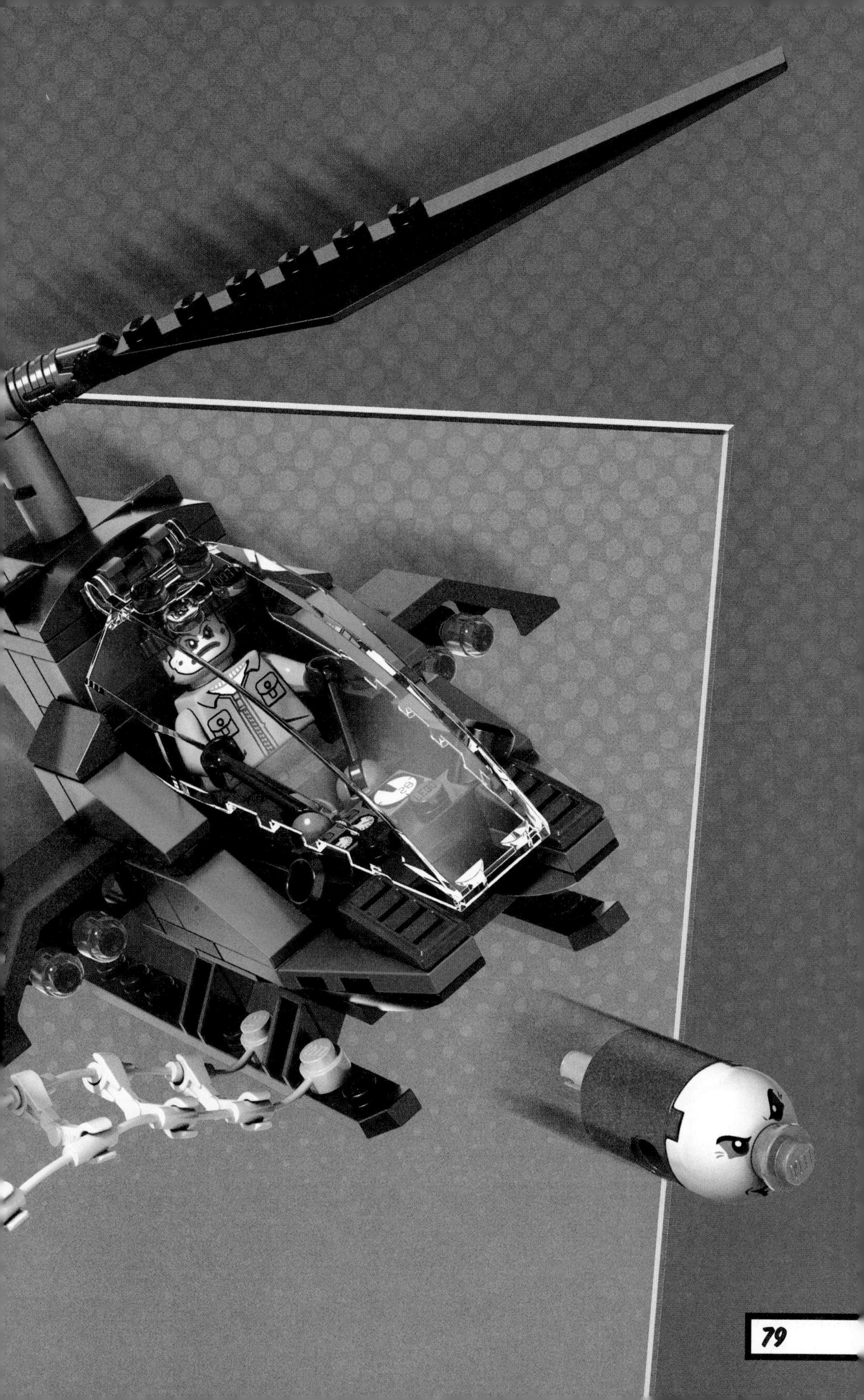

BANE'S DRILL TANK

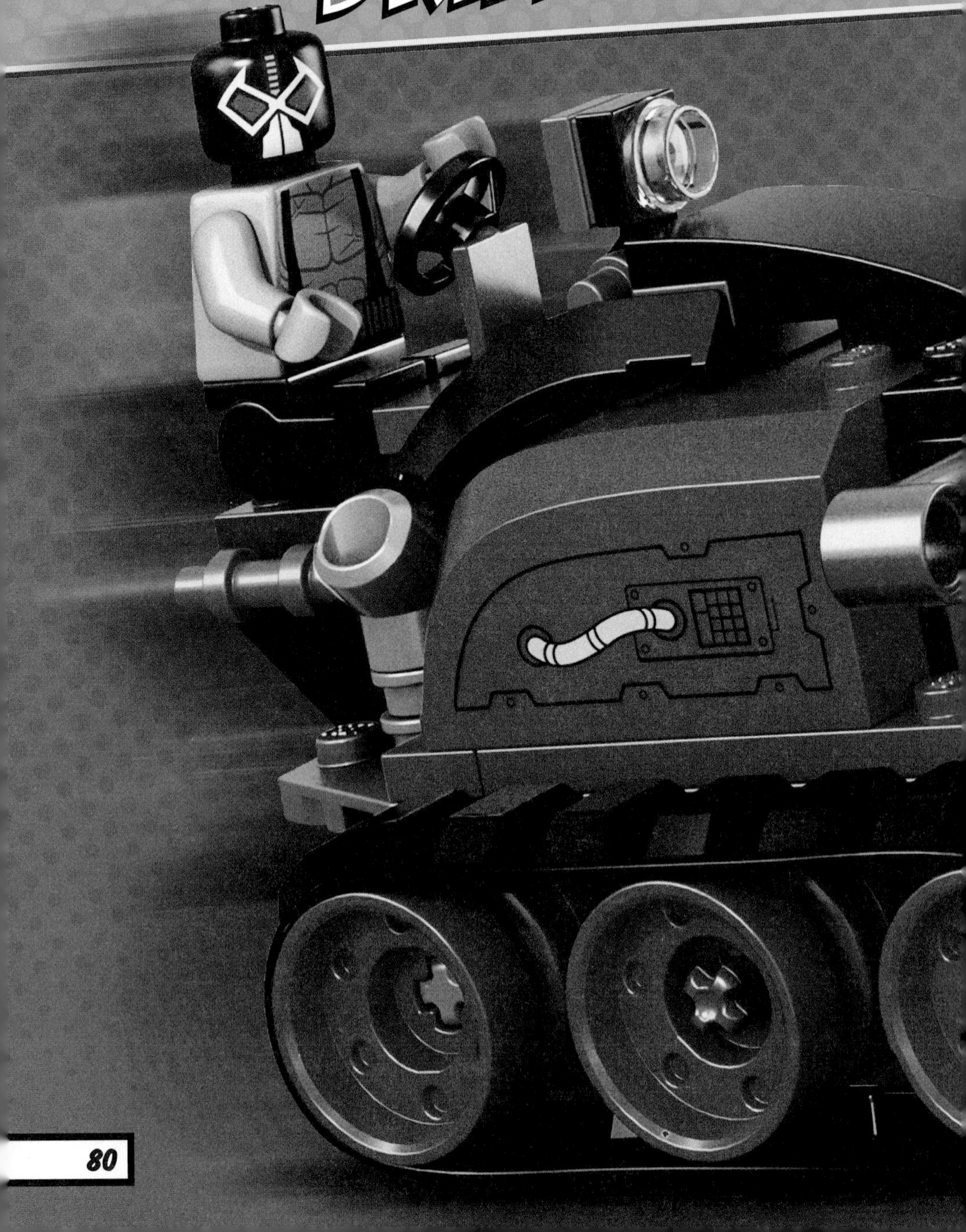

The Drill Tank was originally designed for use by miners. It features a **powerful drill** that can cut through any rock, and also has two **explosive missiles** to blast away any obstacles. Its treads can handle even the toughest terrain. Bane stole the Drill Tank and used it to break into the Batcave, but Batman defeated him.

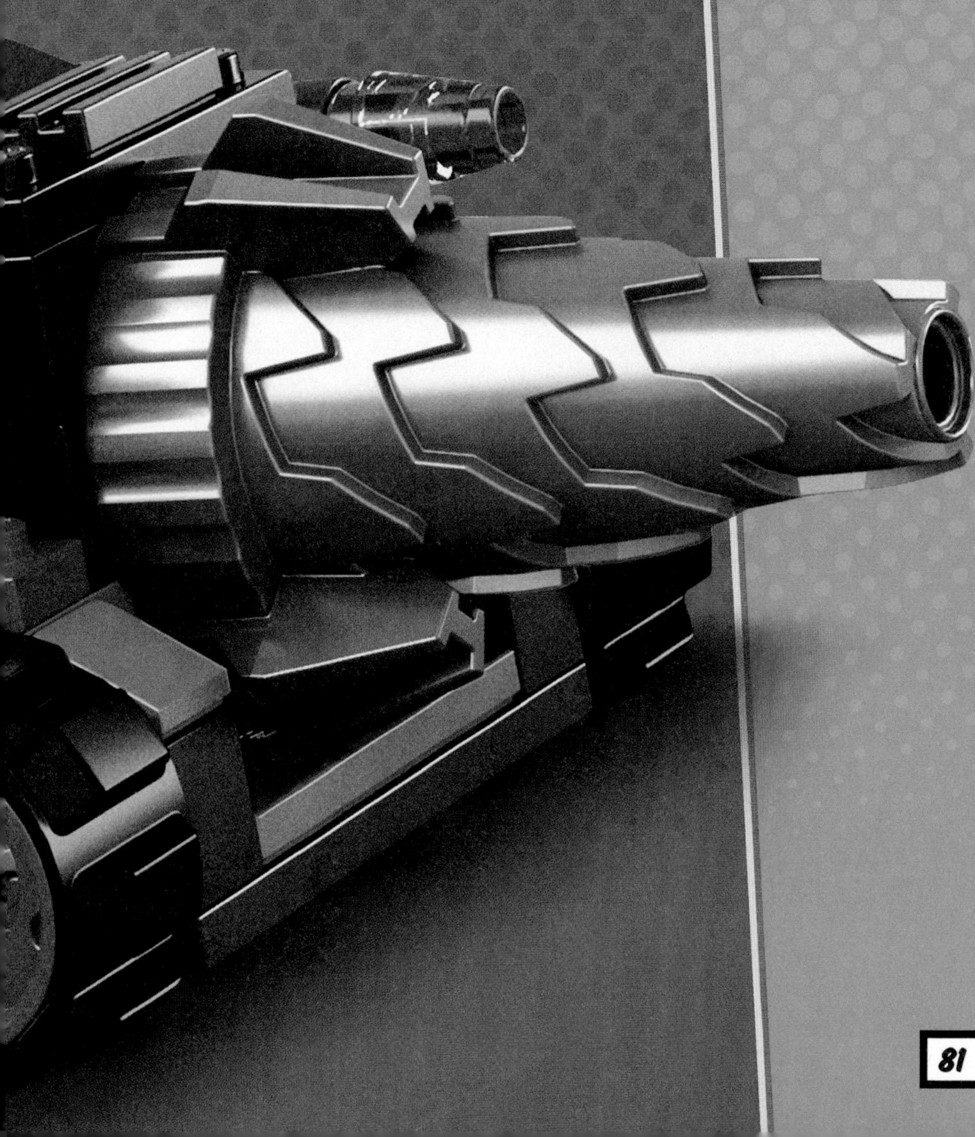

THE TUMBLER

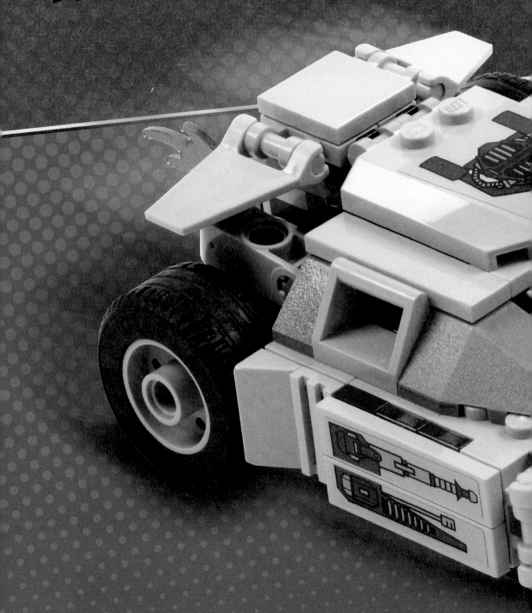

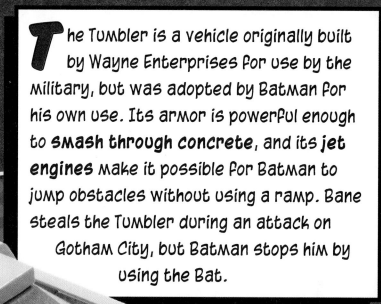

The Tumbler is a vehicle originally built by Wayne Enterprises for use by the military, but was adopted by Batman for his own use. Its armor is powerful enough to **smash through concrete**, and its **jet engines** make it possible for Batman to jump obstacles without using a ramp. Bane steals the Tumbler during an attack on Gotham City, but Batman stops him by using the Bat.

THE CAT-CYCLE

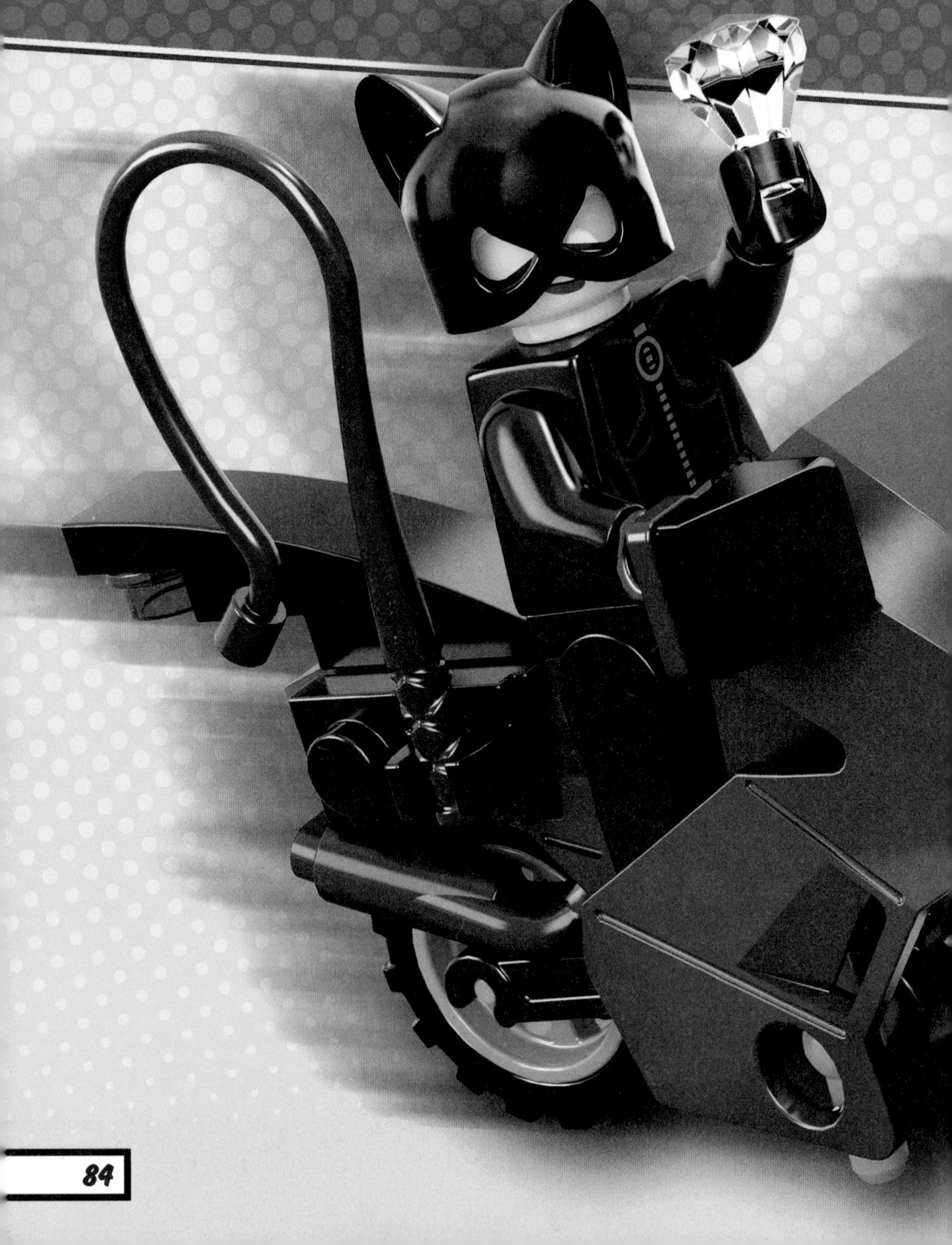

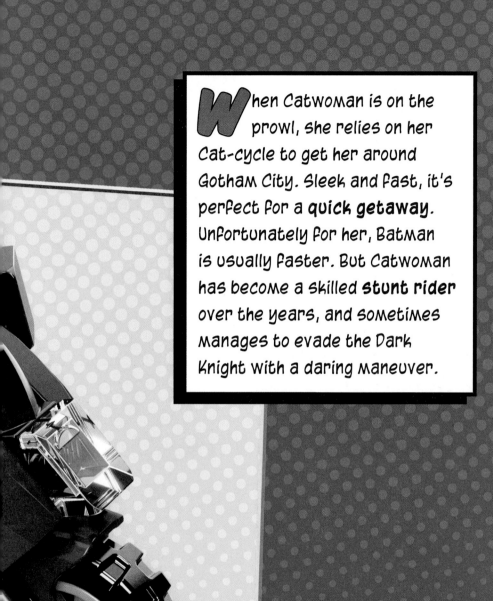

When Catwoman is on the prowl, she relies on her Cat-cycle to get her around Gotham City. Sleek and fast, it's perfect for a **quick getaway**. Unfortunately for her, Batman is usually faster. But Catwoman has become a skilled **stunt rider** over the years, and sometimes manages to evade the Dark Knight with a daring maneuver.

TWO-FACE'S TOW TRUCK

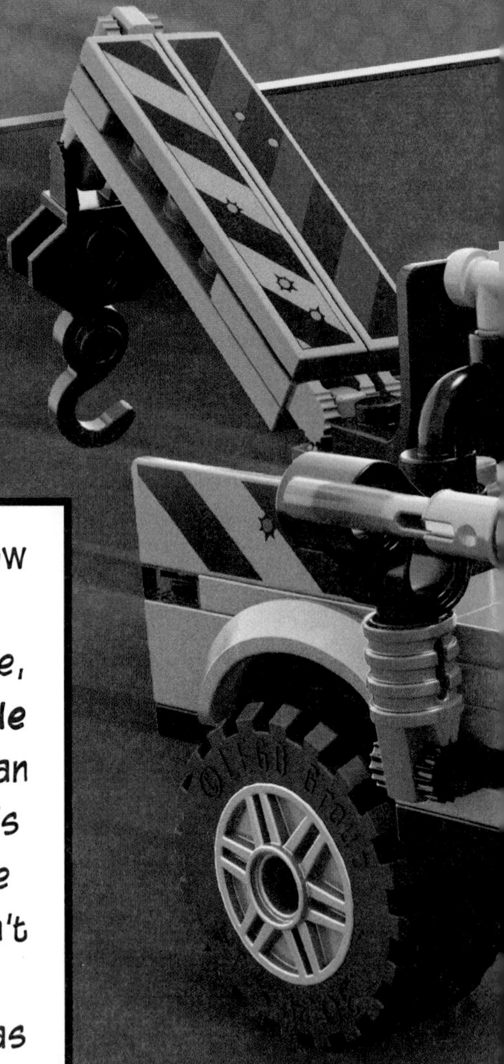

Two-Face stole this tow truck, had it painted half purple and half orange, and armed it with a **missile** and a **machine gun**. His plan was to use the tow truck's **arm** to haul away the safe from the bank. But he didn't count on the Batmobile, which was twice as fast as his ride.

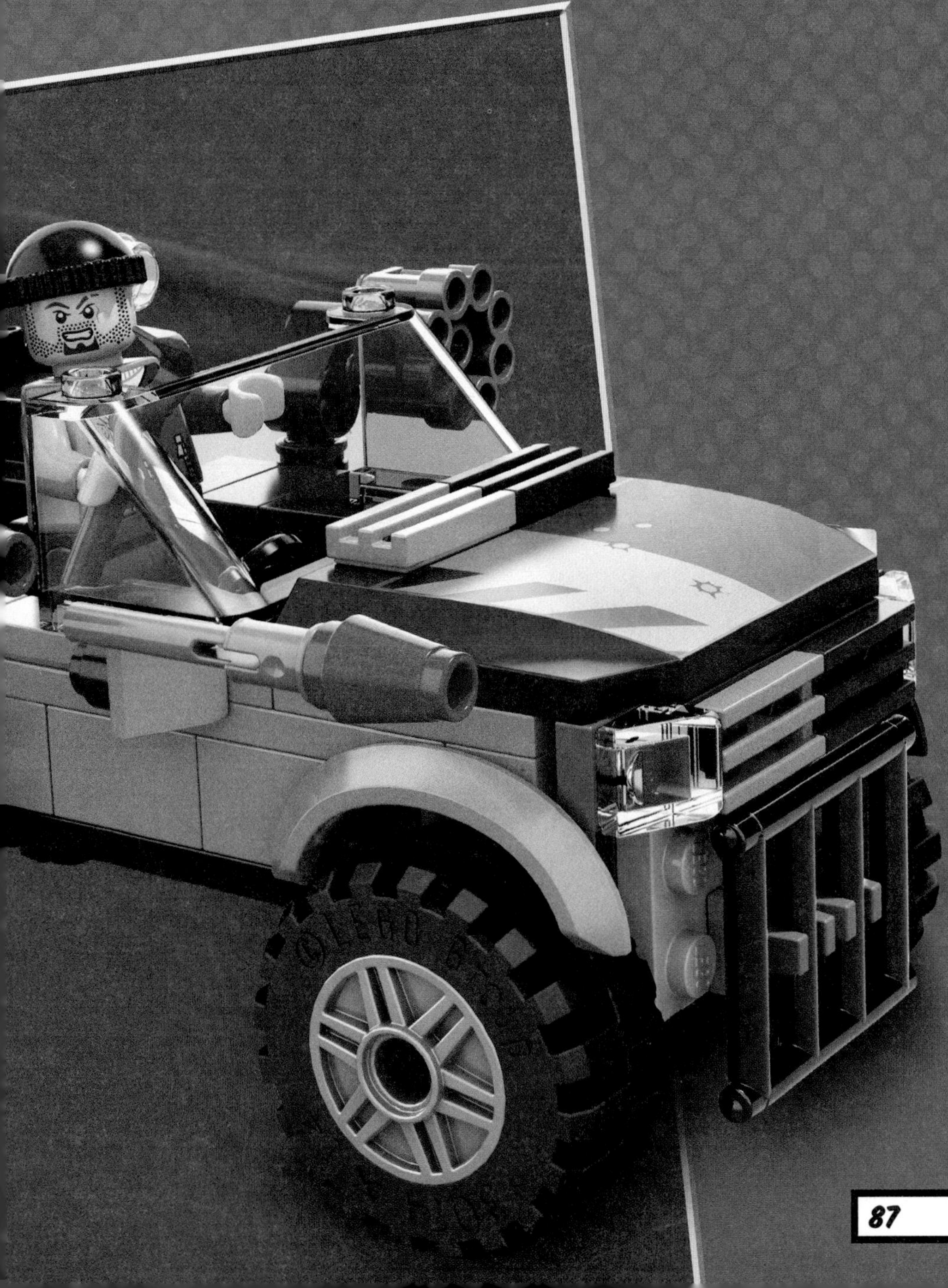

ARKHAM ASYLUM SECURITY VAN

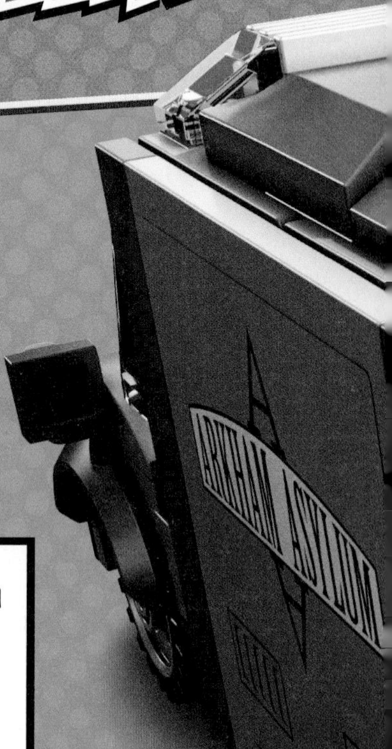
ARKHAM ASYLUM
GOTHAM CITY

The Arkham Asylum security van is a **heavily armored** vehicle designed to take prisoners from Gotham City Jail to Arkham Asylum. It's equipped with a powerful **radio** and an **alarm** that signals Police Headquarters. Despite all this, prisoners seem to keep escaping from it. Sometimes, they even steal it to make their getaway!

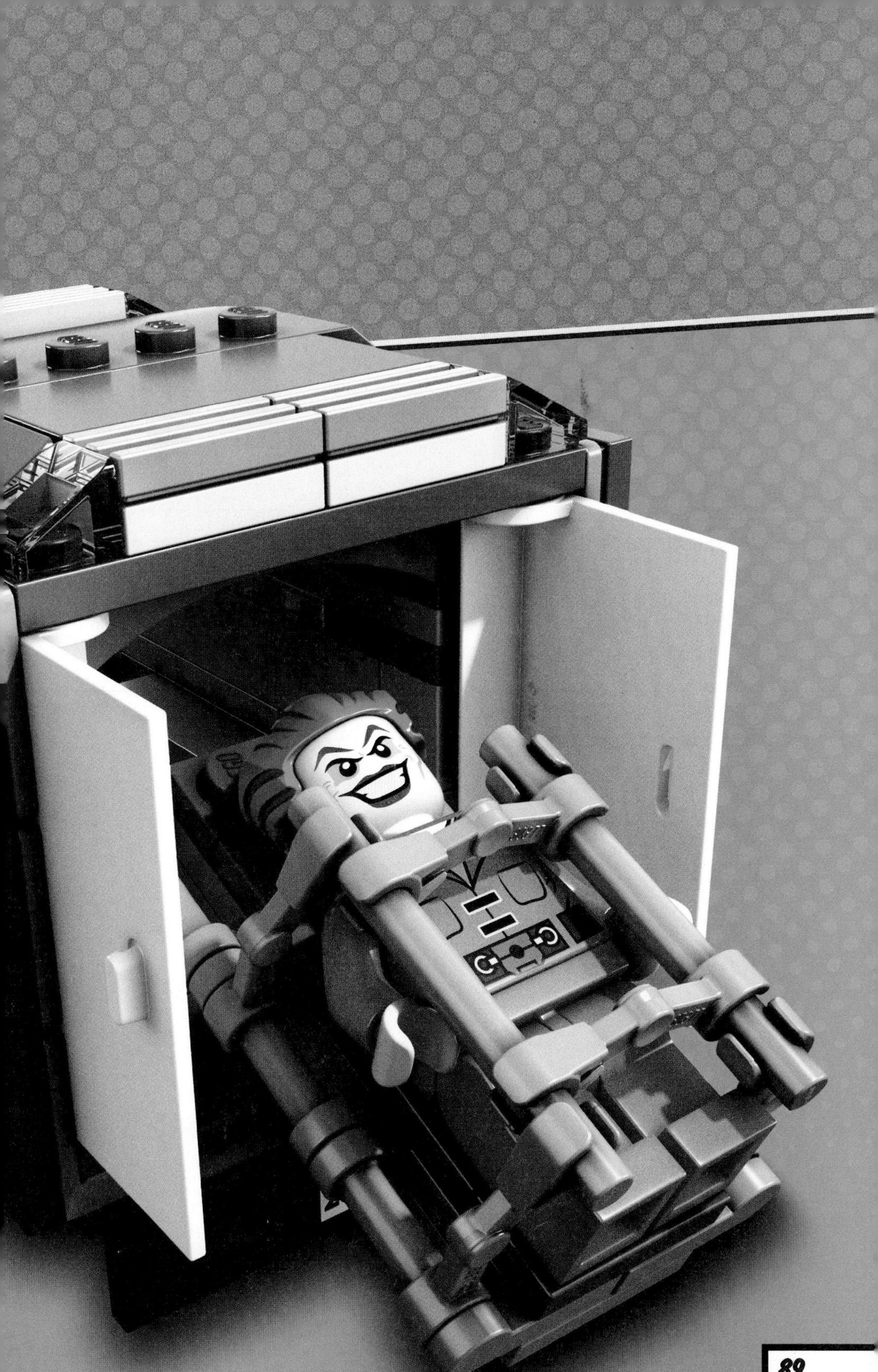

POWER ARMOR

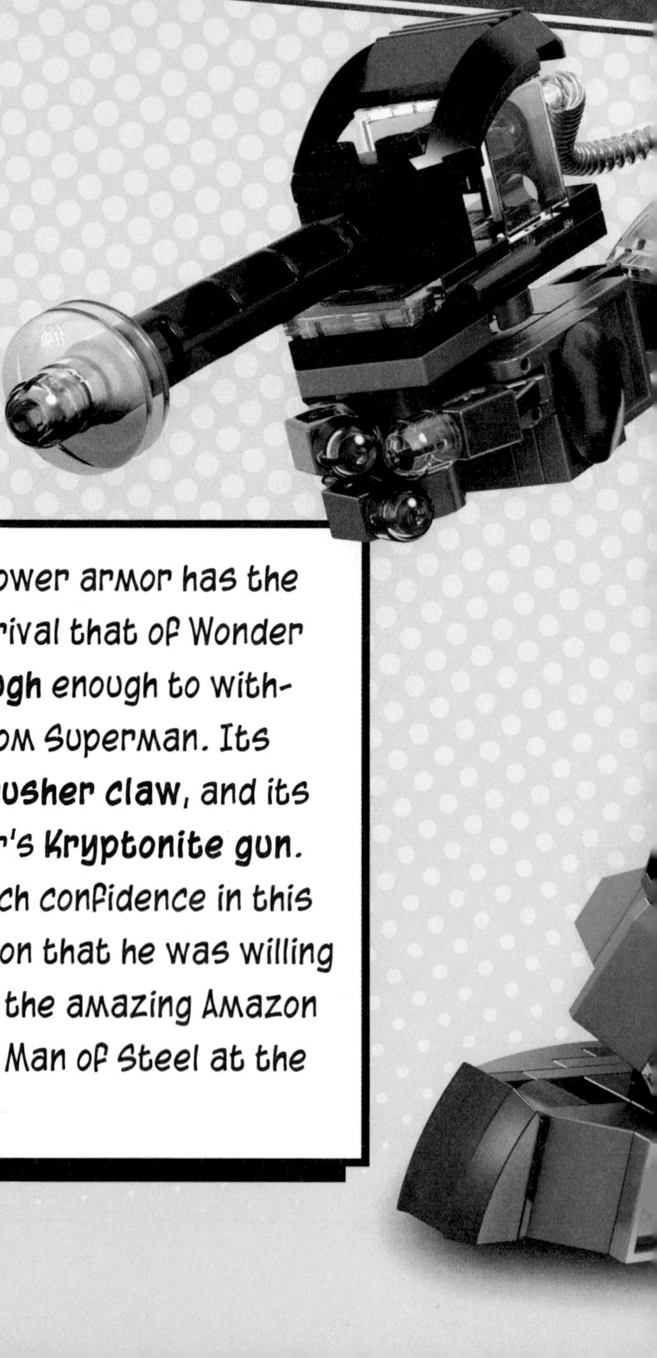

Lex Luthor's power armor has the **strength** to rival that of Wonder Woman and is **tough** enough to withstand a punch from Superman. Its left arm has a **crusher claw**, and its right holds Luthor's **Kryptonite gun**. Luthor has so much confidence in this incredible invention that he was willing to use it against the amazing Amazon Princess and the Man of Steel at the same time!

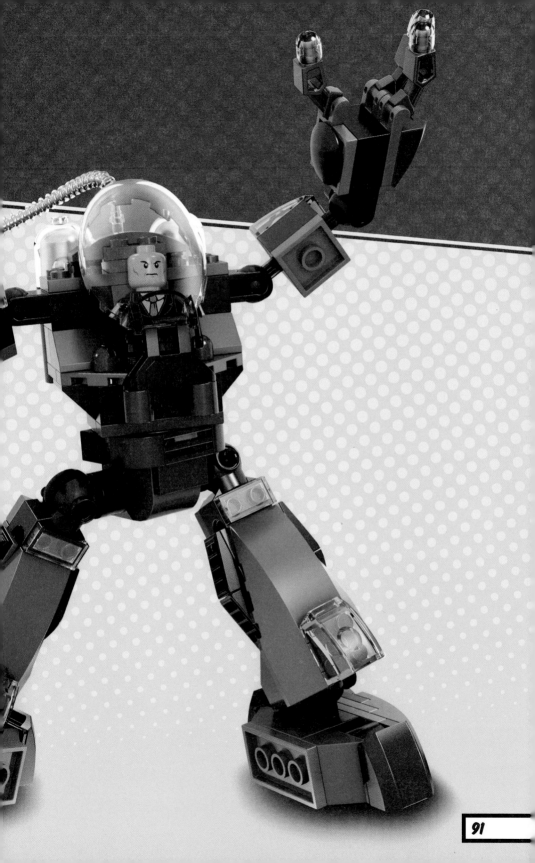

OFF-ROADER

Colonel Hardy's off-roader is a military vehicle equipped with a rear-mounted **multi-missile launcher**. Fast and able to tackle tough terrain, Hardy uses it in the battle of Smallville against Zod and his Kryptonian henchmen. But can any human weapon stop rampaging Kryptonians? The off-roader features special **puncture-proof** tires and extra **armor plating** on its body.

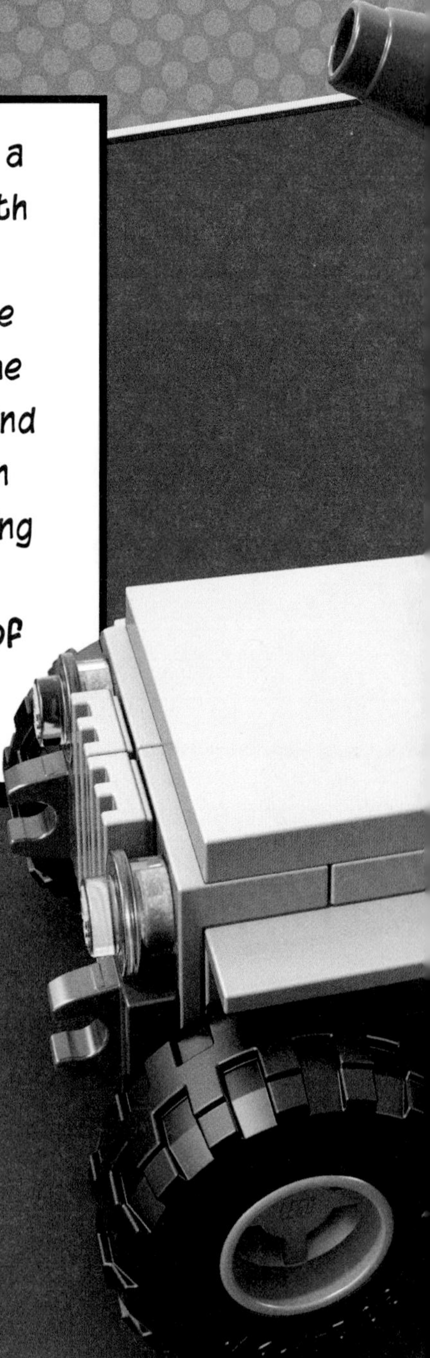

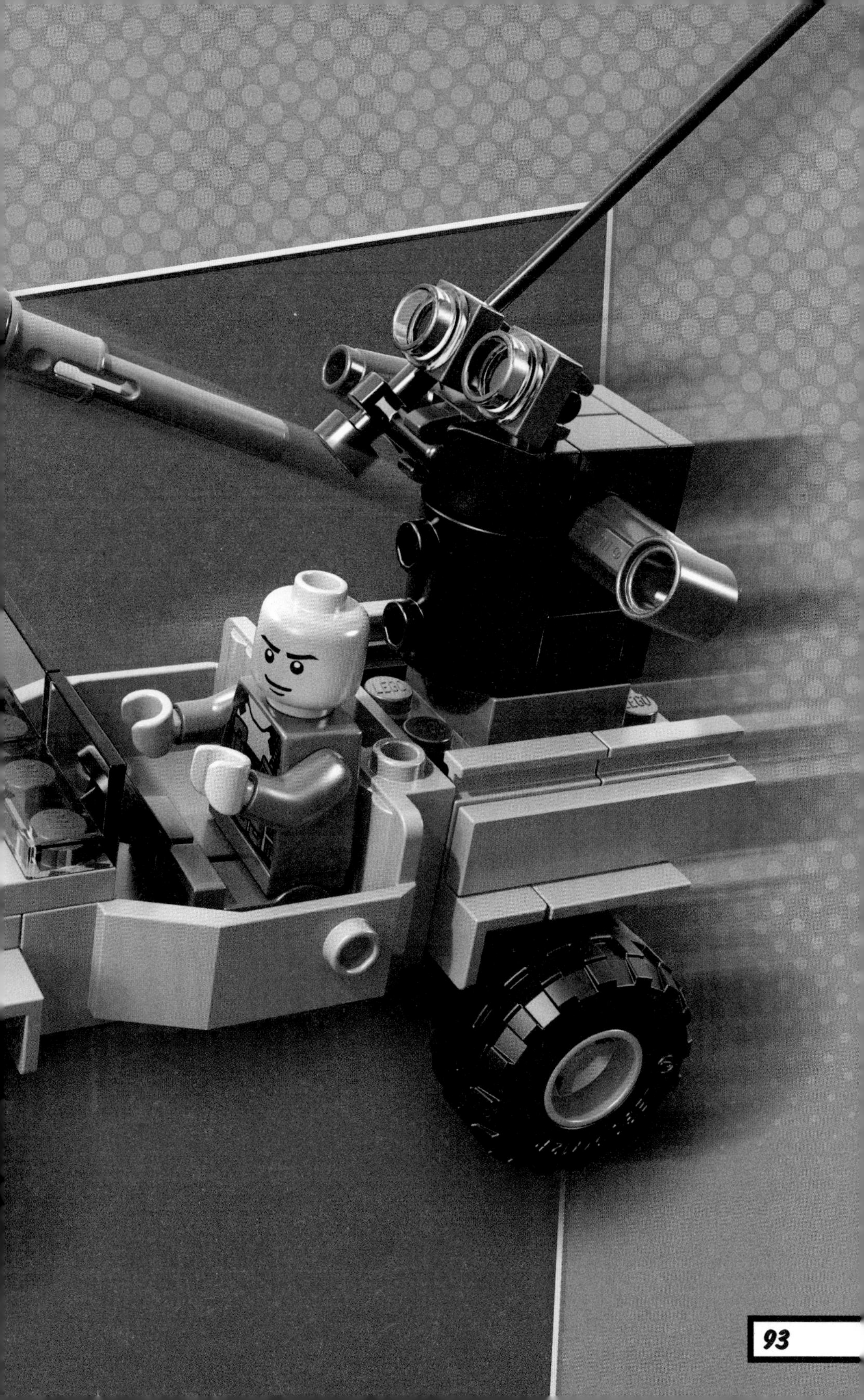

BLACK ZERO DROP SHIP

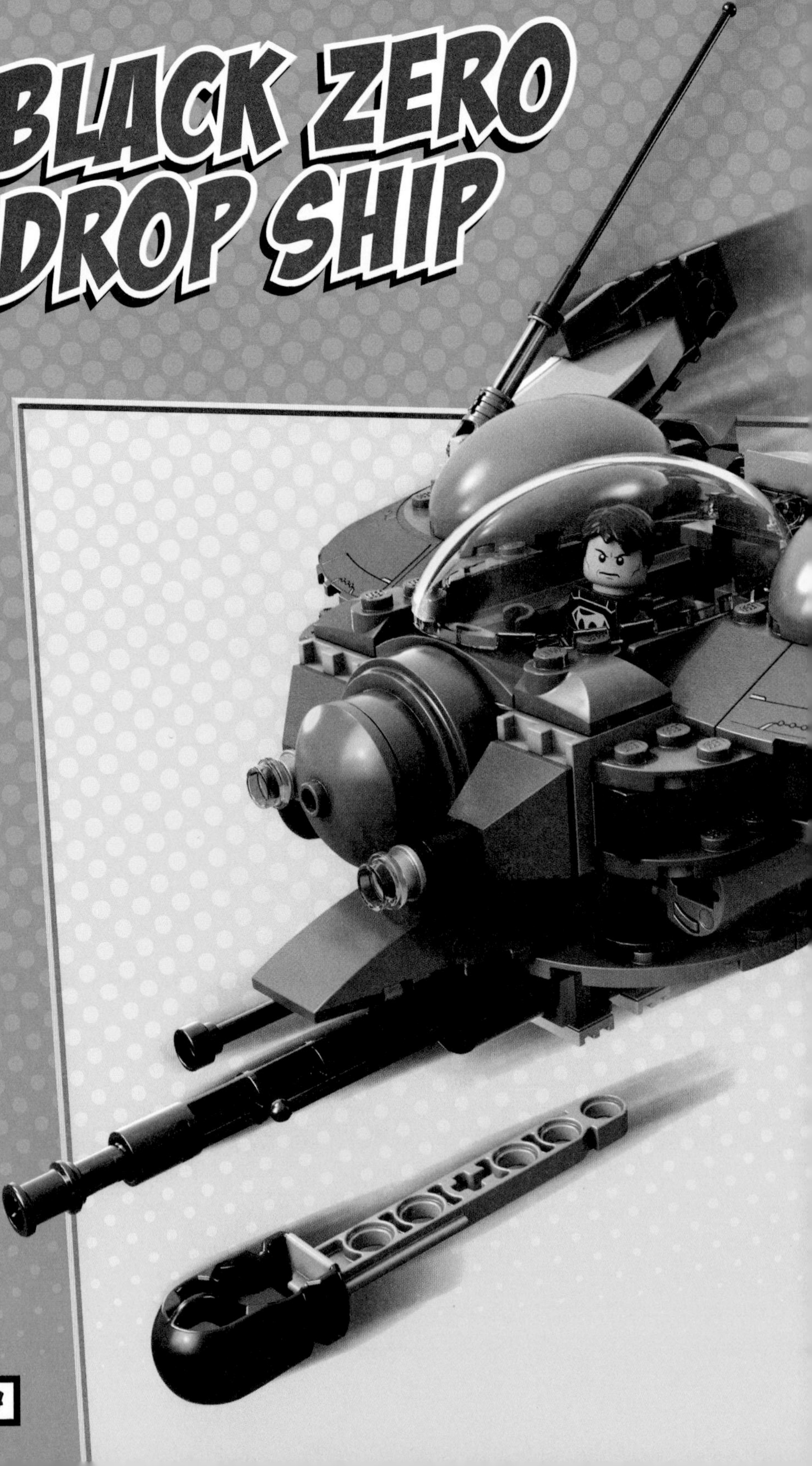

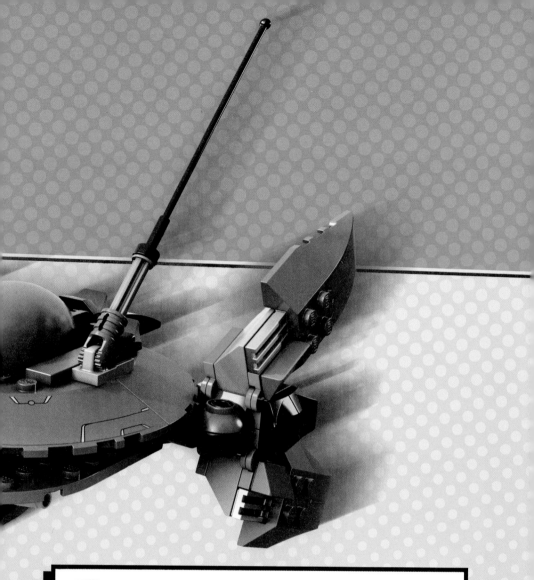

This sleek craft is capable of operating both in space and in the atmosphere. Piloted by General Zod, it is armed with **missiles** and packs a powerful punch that can rock even the Man of Steel. Zod intends to use it to conquer Earth. Built using Kryptonian technology, its **hull armor** is impervious even to the power of Superman.

BLACK ZERO ESCAPE POD

This escape pod is designed for use in emergencies. It features multiple **rocket engines** that can be steered from within the cockpit so that it can change direction as needed. Its Kryptonian **armored hull** makes it invulnerable to Earth weapons and in most cases would allow it to escape a crash onto the planet's surface. Lois Lane, however, would prefer not to find out what will happen when it hits the ground with her in it. . . .

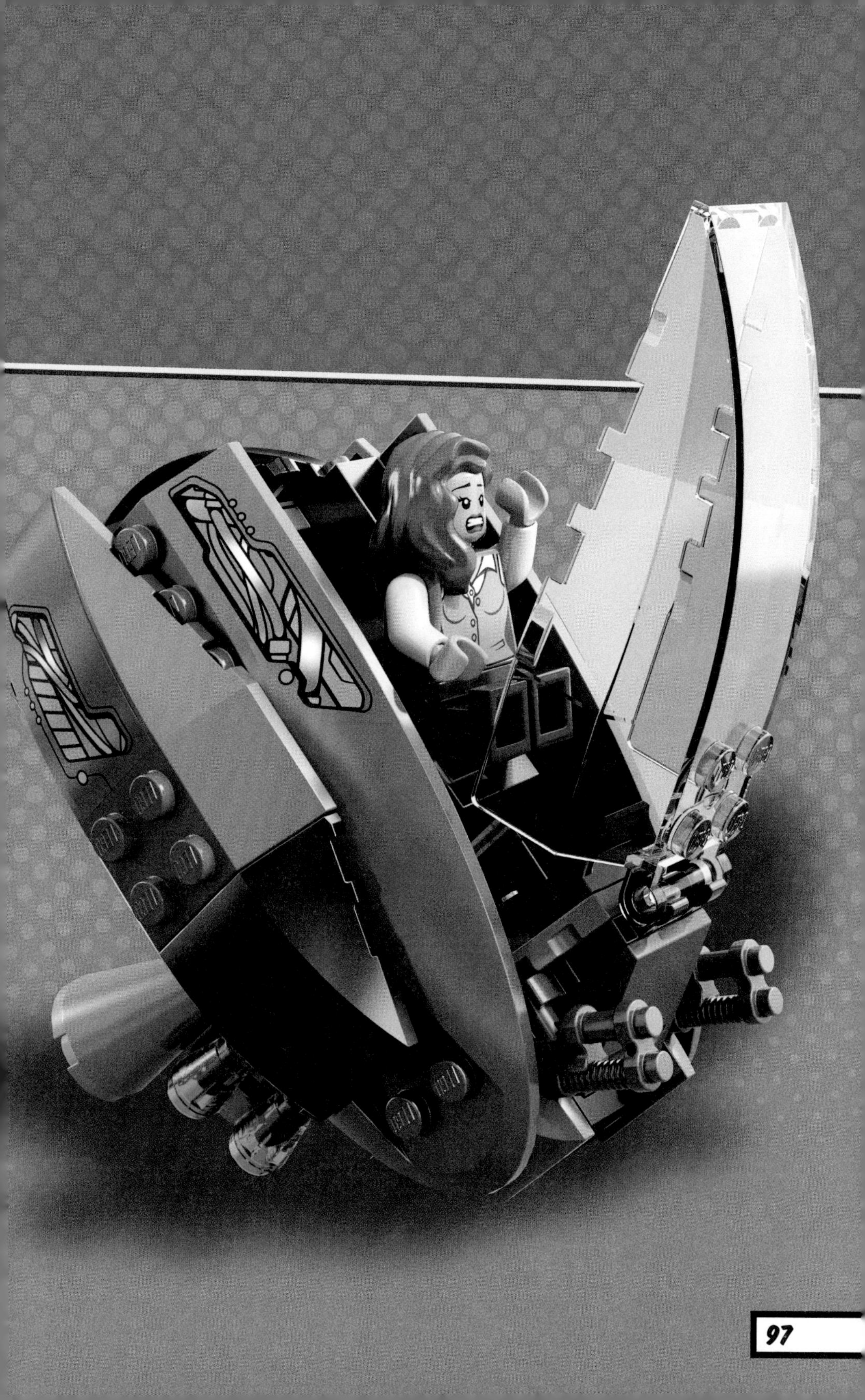

CHAPTER 4
LOCATIONS!

THE LEGO DC UNIVERSE IS FILLED WITH PLACES THAT ARE EXCITING, MYSTERIOUS, AND DANGEROUS. IN ANY CORNER OF THE WORLD, YOU MIGHT FIND A SUPER HERO'S SECRET BASE OR THE HIDDEN HIDEOUT OF A MASTER VILLAIN. ALTHOUGH A HERO OR VILLAIN MIGHT BE NORMALLY SEEN IN ONE CITY, THEY OFTEN TRAVEL ELSEWHERE. SO DON'T BE SURPRISED TO SEE WONDER WOMAN IN METROPOLIS OR AQUAMAN IN GOTHAM CITY!

GOTHAM CITY

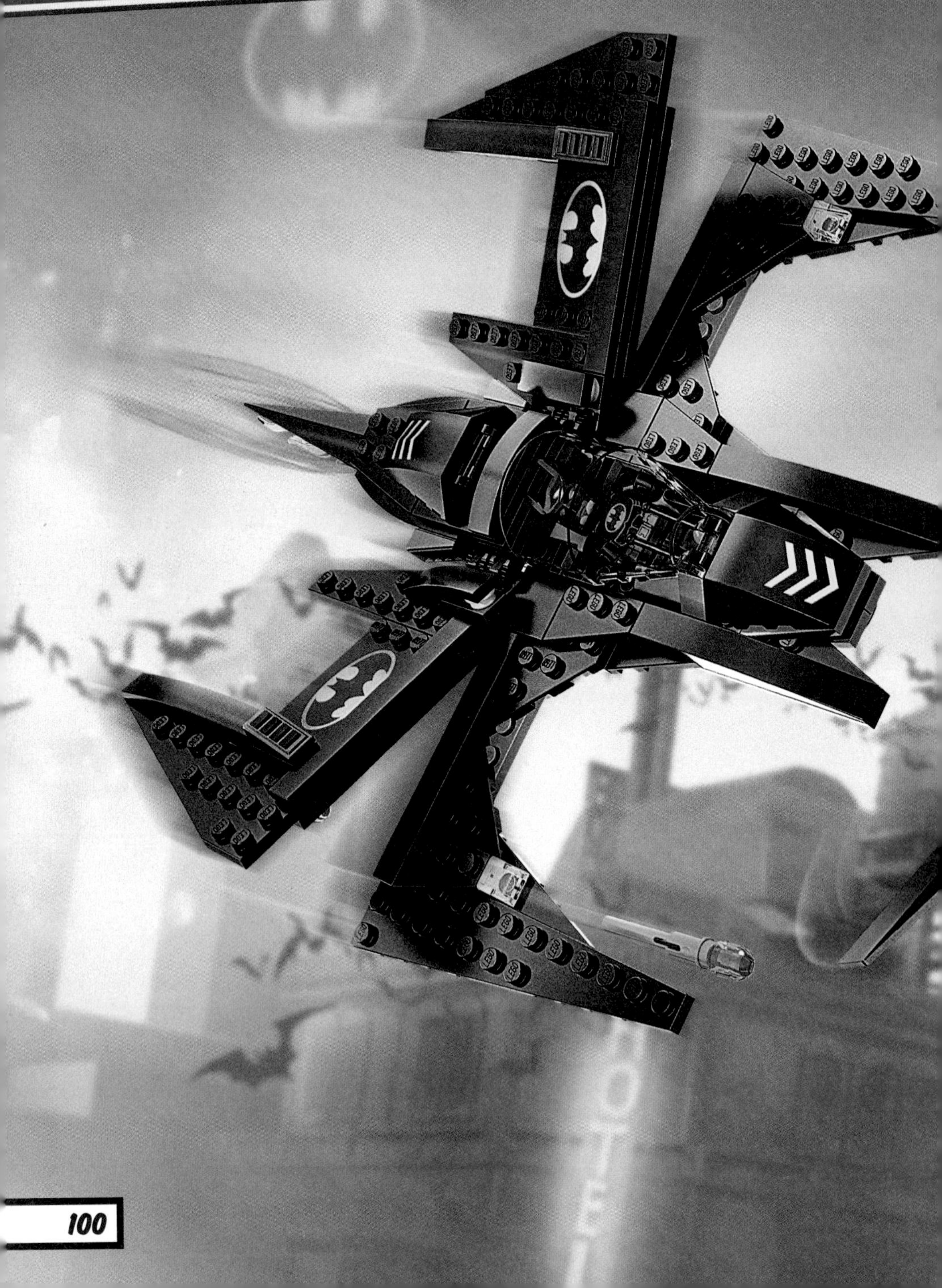

Gotham City is the home city of **Batman** and **Robin**. It is also home to a number of super-villains and a lot of **crime**, so Batman is always busy. Gotham City was, at one time, a thriving place, but it has fallen on hard times. That is why there are so many abandoned factories and warehouses for super-villains to use as **hideouts**.

Some of the famous sites in Gotham City include the Wayne Enterprises building, Robinson Park, Gotham Heights, Wayne Manor, Gotham Stadium, and Arkham Asylum.

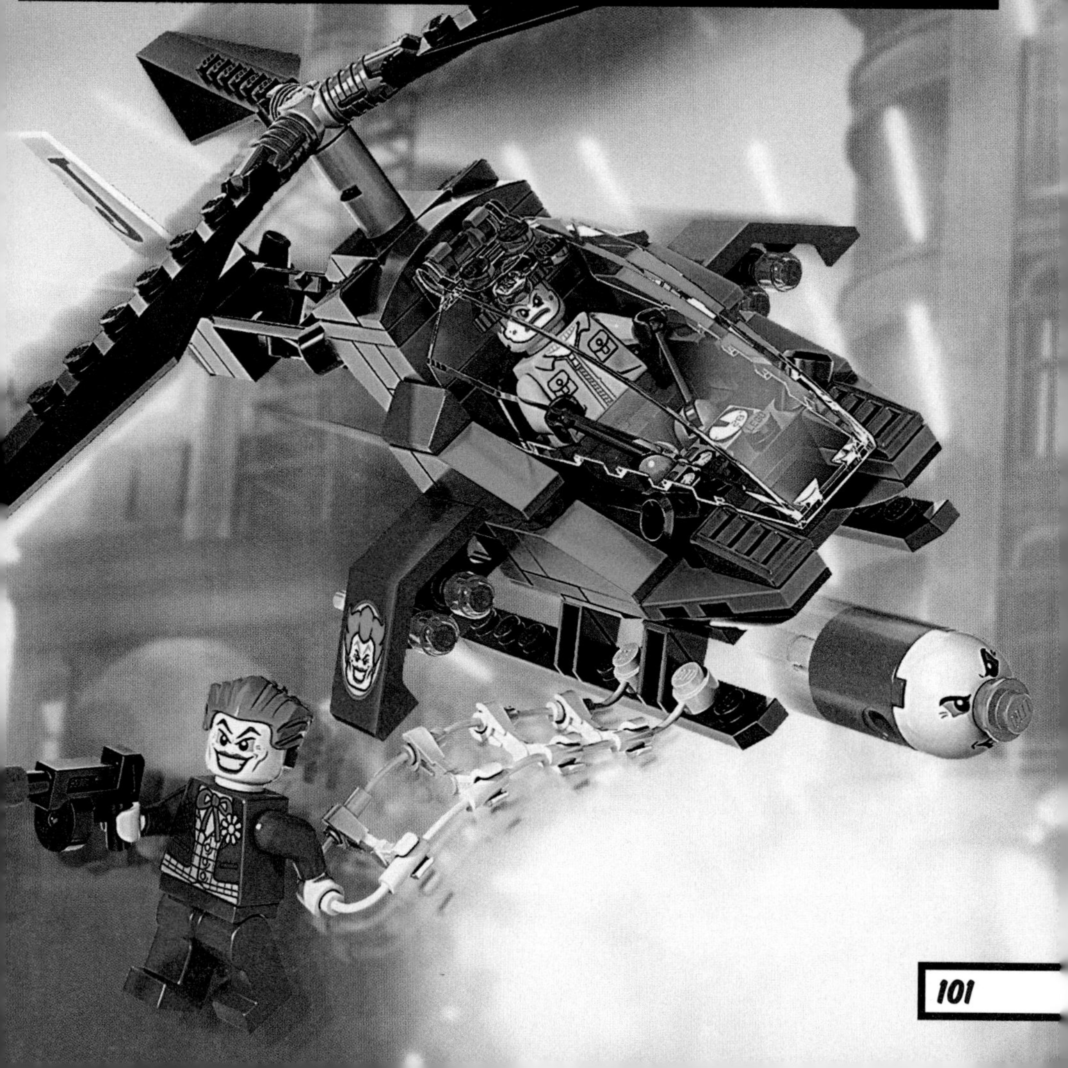

METROPOLIS

Metropolis is one of the largest and most famous cities in the DC Universe, because it is the home of **Superman**. Metropolis is a much more **modern** city than Gotham City, with glass-and-steel skyscrapers everywhere as well as the *Daily Planet* Building. Superman works for the *Daily Planet* in his other identity of Clark Kent.

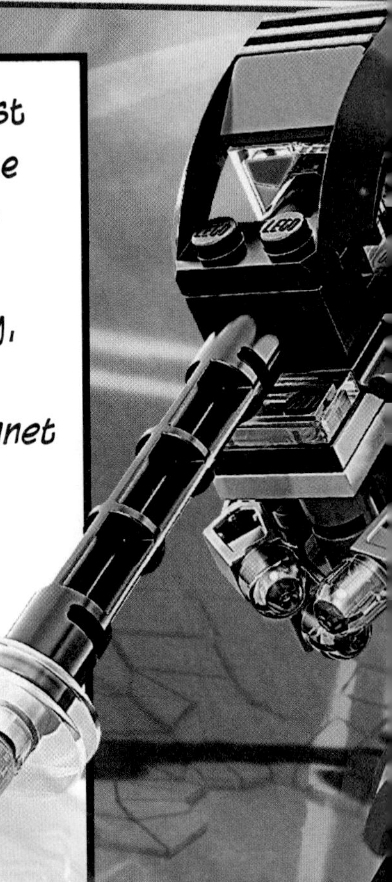

Metropolis sees its share of action, with **alien invaders** and super-villains often showing up there to take on the Man of Steel. Fortunately, Superman is able to rapidly repair any damage done to the city by his battles.

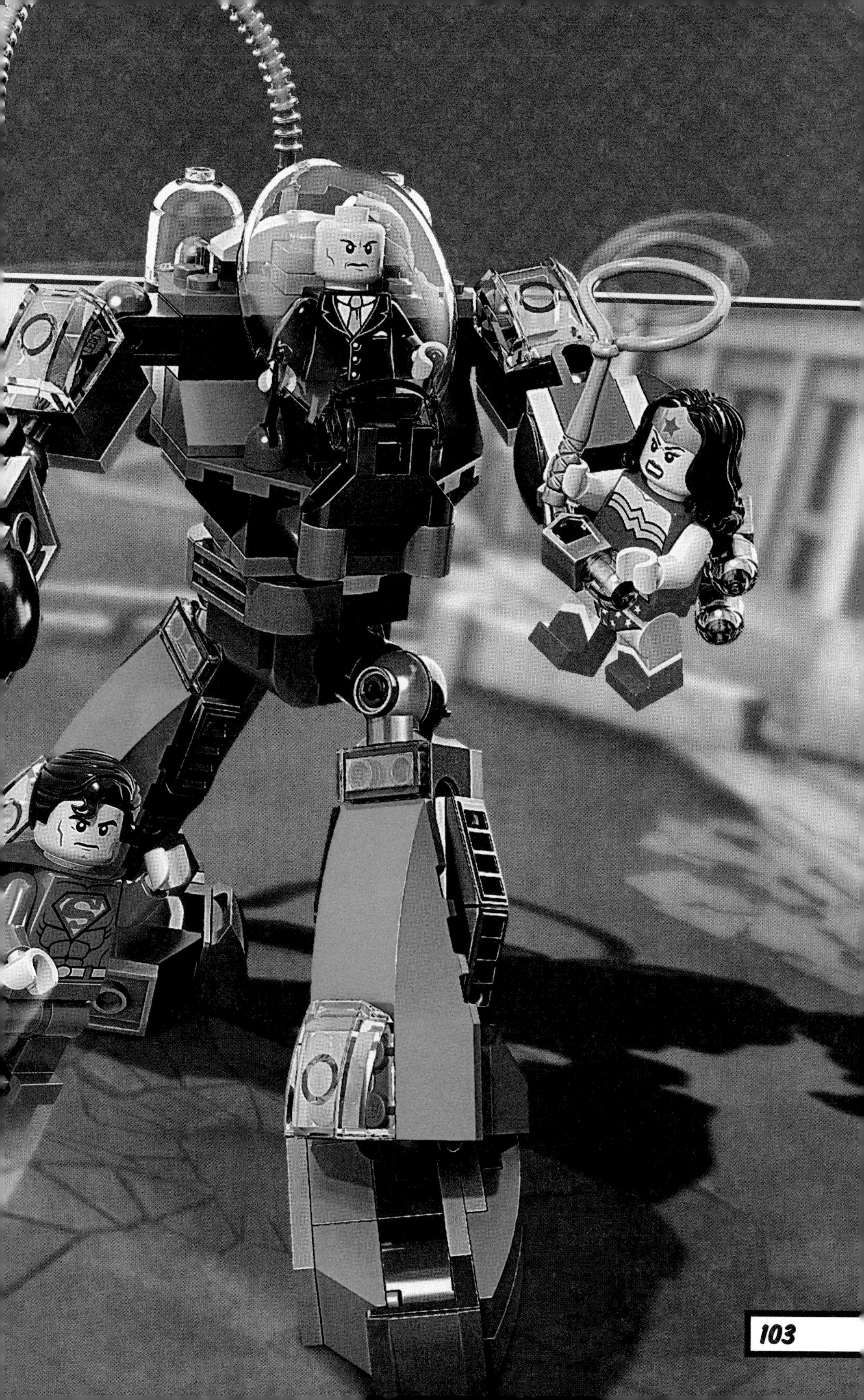

THE BATCAVE

Batman's and Robin's **secret headquarters**, the Batcave, is located beneath Wayne Manor in Gotham City. Batman has filled it with everything he needs for his fight against crime, from the **Batcomputer** to a special elevator for costume changes and a **holding cell** for dangerous prisoners like Poison Ivy. Batman also keeps his awesome vehicles here, including the Batcycle. The location of the Batcave is a closely guarded secret, but at least one Batman villain—Bane—has found it in the past.

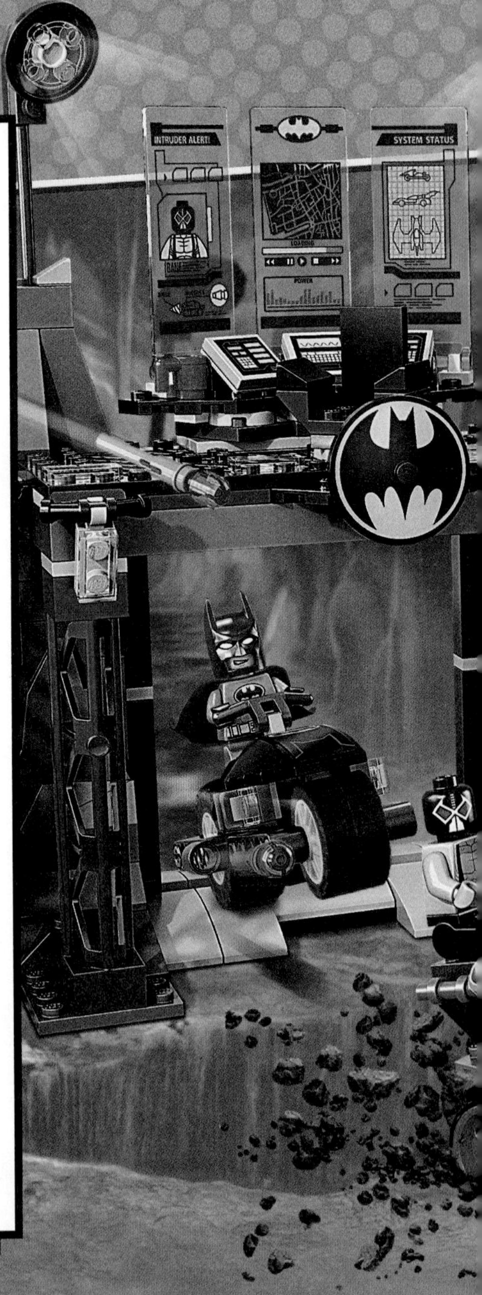

INTRUDER ALERT!
SYSTEM STATUS

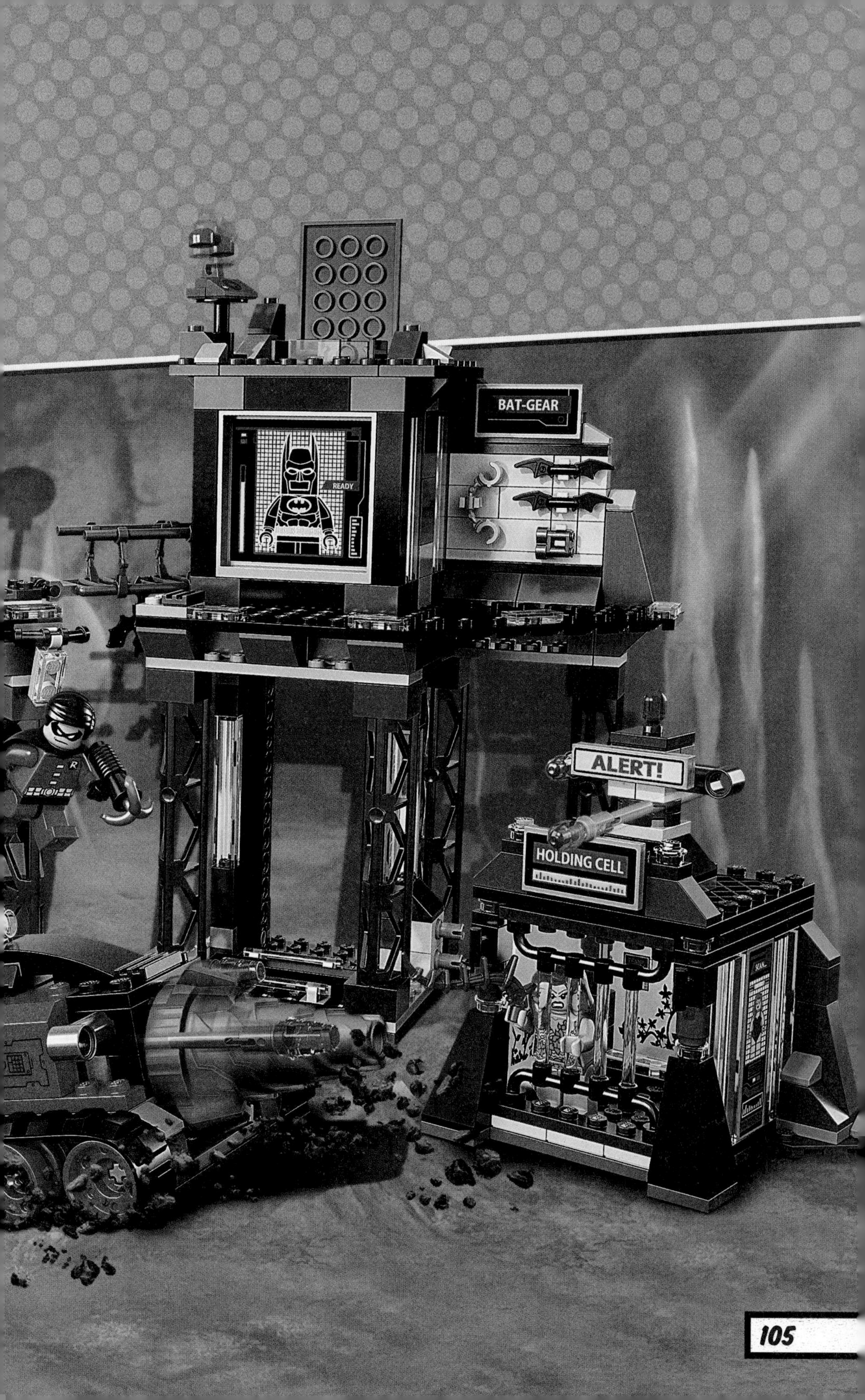
BAT-GEAR
READY
ALERT!
HOLDING CELL

THE FUNHOUSE

The Joker, Harley Quinn, and the Riddler have taken over this long-abandoned amusement park attraction as part of a plot to trap Batman and Robin. They have rigged the place with assorted **dangerous traps**, including a **giant hammer**, numerous **trap-doors**, and **floors that move** under the Dark Knight's feet. Everything is set up to make this place anything but "fun" for the Dynamic Duo—but before the fight is over, the joke may be on the Joker!

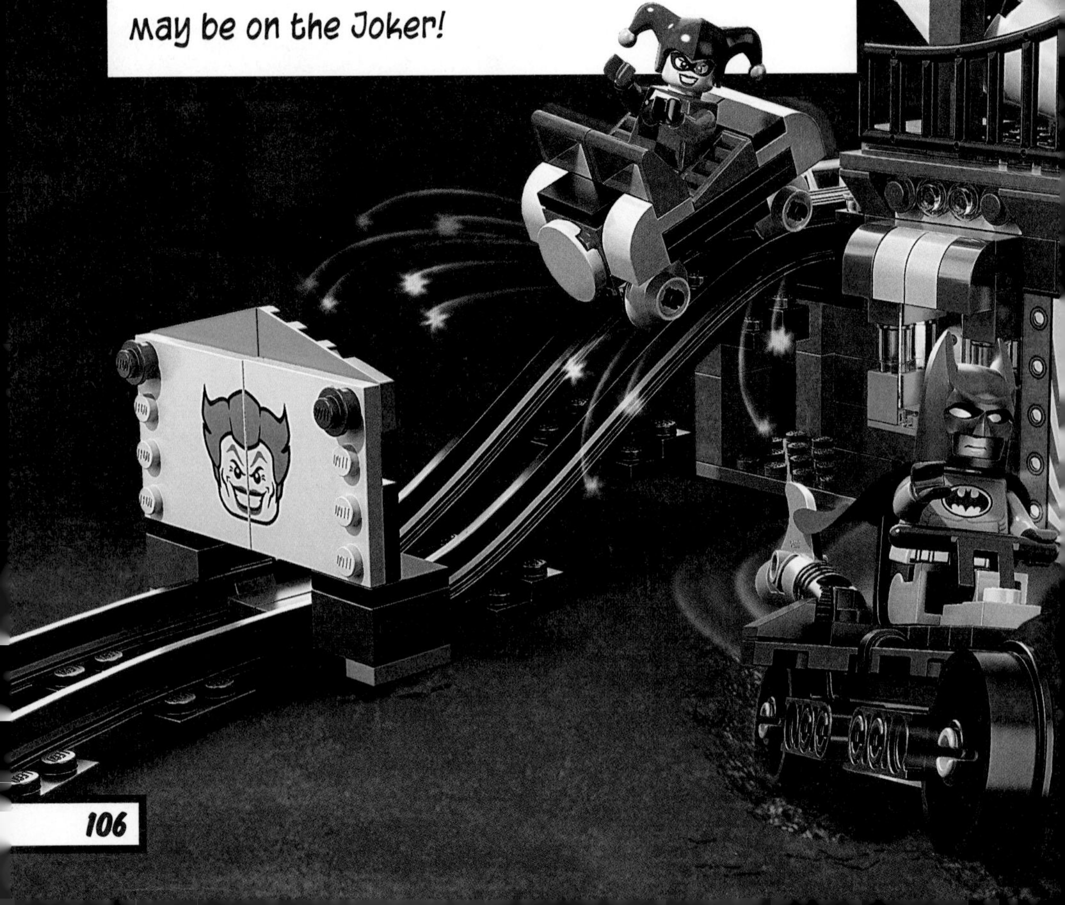

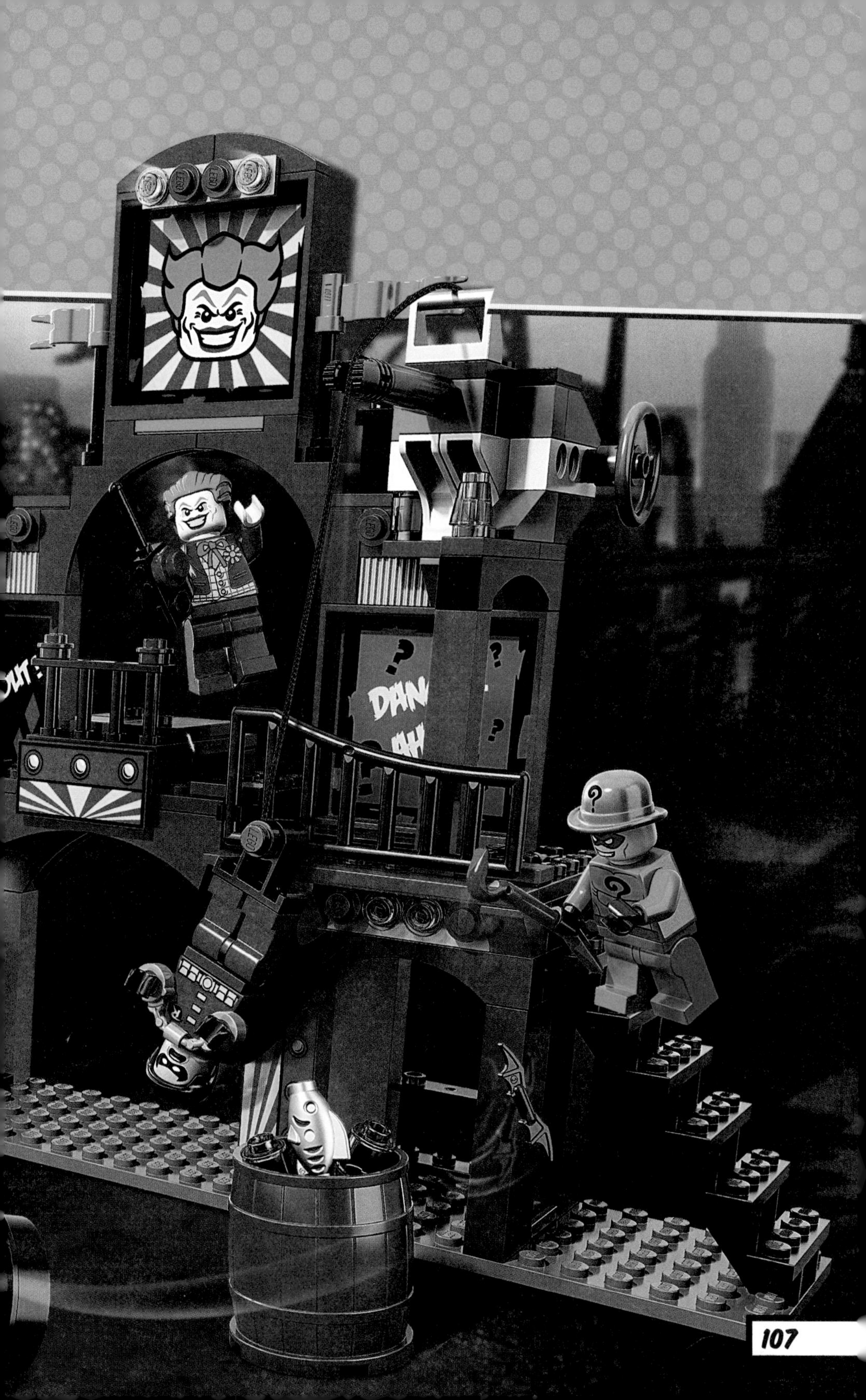

ARKHAM ASYLUM

This home for the **criminally insane** is located on the outskirts of Gotham City. In the past, it has served as a **prison** for villains like the Joker, the Scarecrow, Poison Ivy, and more. Unfortunately, no matter how tight the security is, the dangerous felons always seem to be able to escape and rampage through Gotham City again. The asylum features unique cells for the different villains housed there, its own **fleet** of security vans, and **armed guards** who are supposed to prevent escapes.

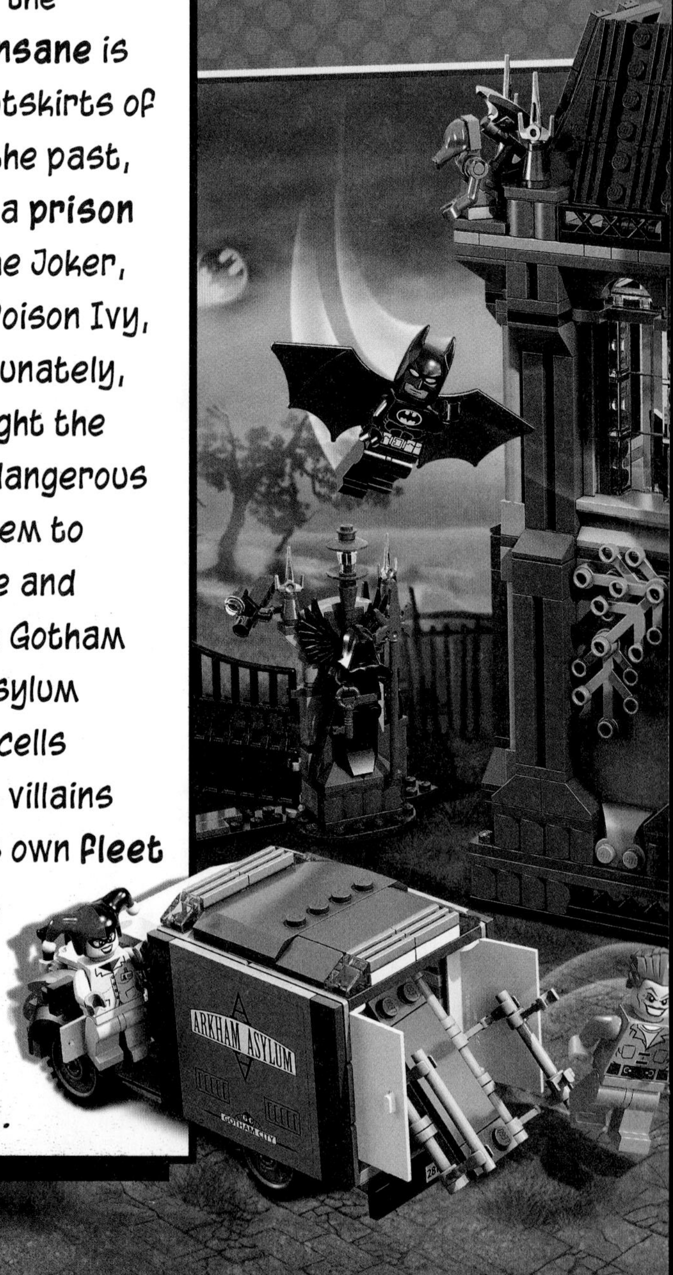
ARKHAM ASYLUM
GOTHAM CITY

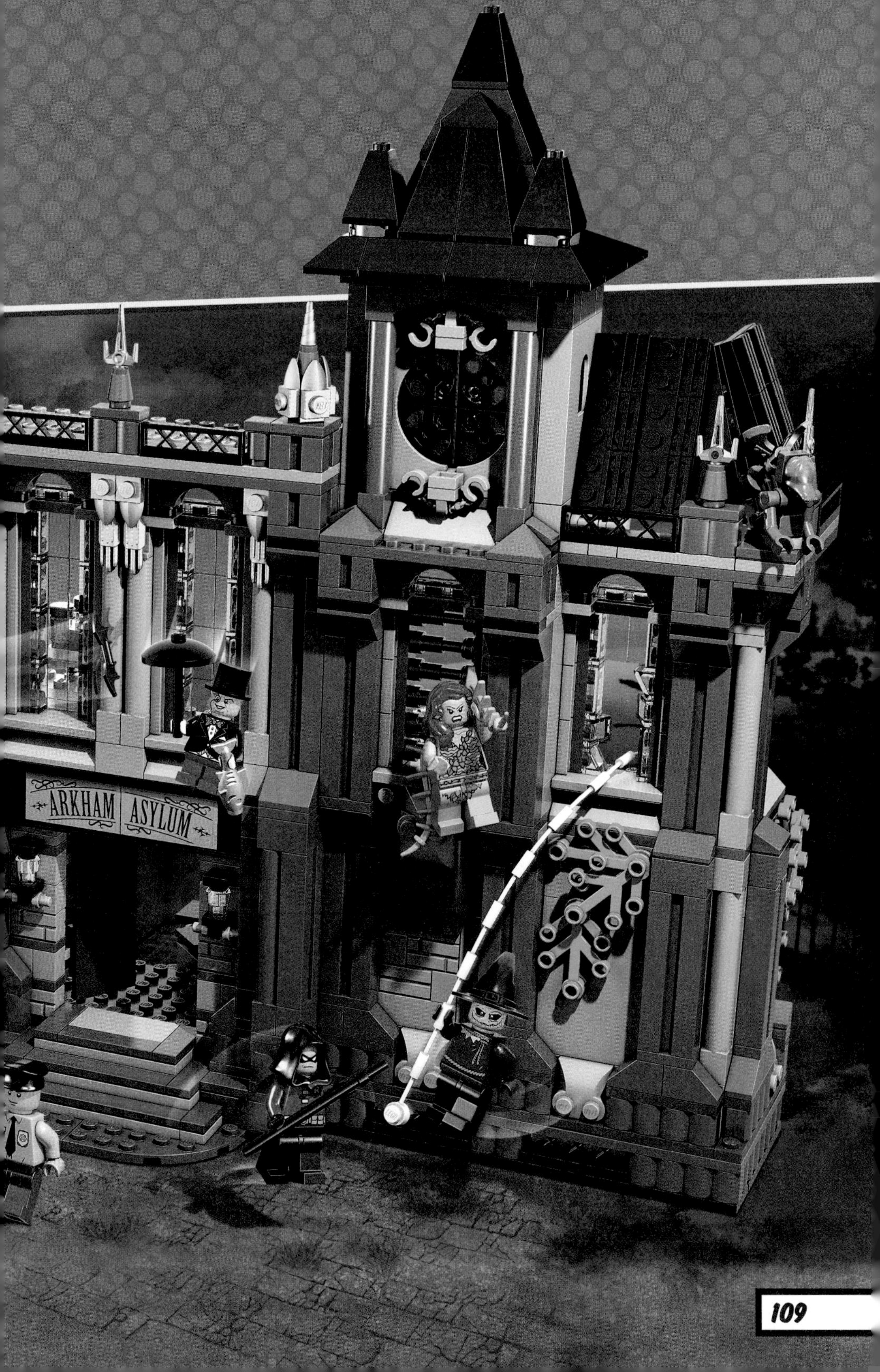
ARKHAM ASYLUM

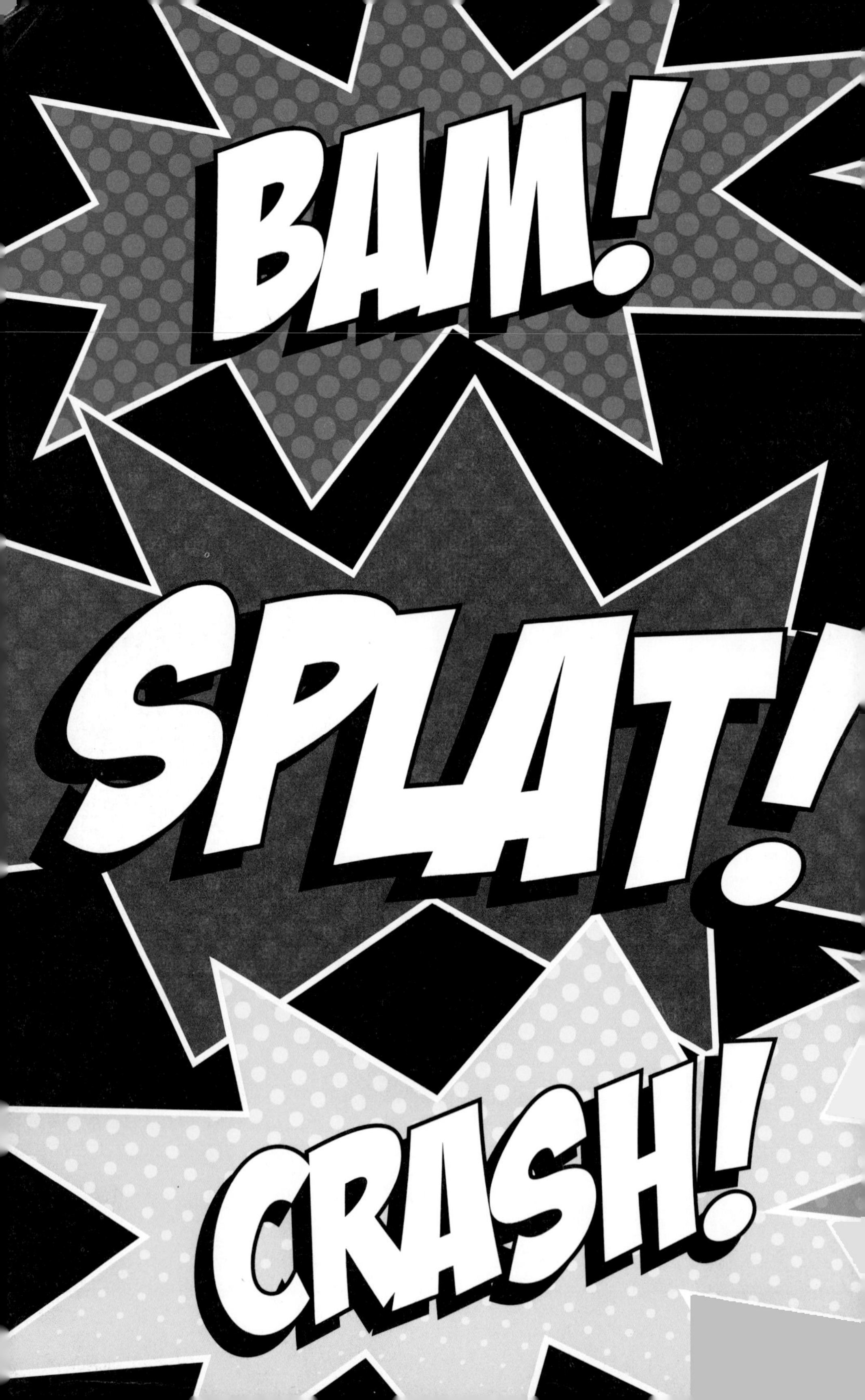
BAM!
SPLAT!
CRASH!

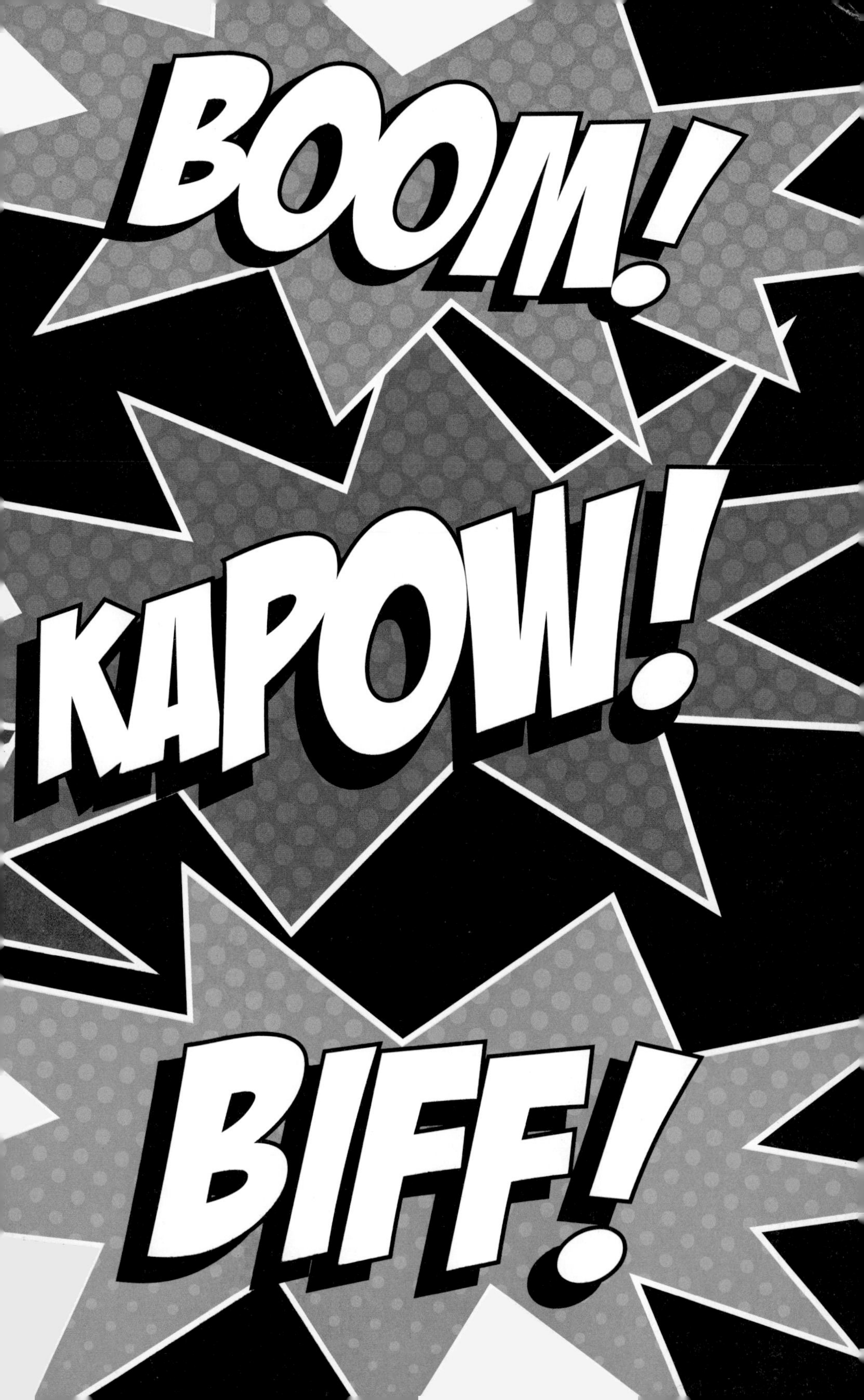
BOOM!
KAPOW!
BIFF!

THE END

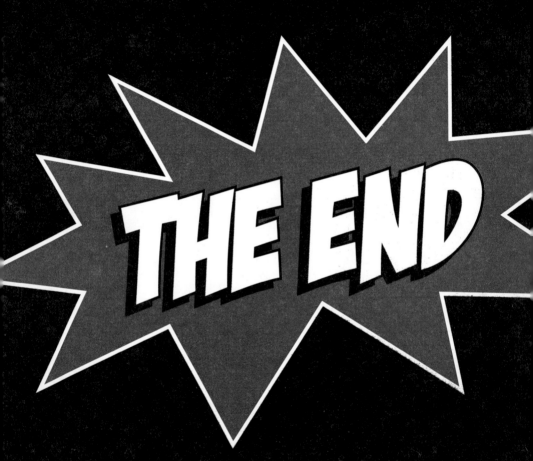